CHIMERA

ELISE NOBLE

Published by Undercover Publishing Limited

Copyright © 2022 Elise Noble

v2

ISBN: 978-1-912888-52-8

Edited by Nikki Mentges, NAM Editorial

Cover design by Abigail Sins

www.undercover-publishing.com

www.elise-noble.com

Monsters are the darkness inside us.

— EMMY BLACK

1

EMMY

"You eat it."

"No, you eat it." I shoved the plate of haggis back across the table to Sky. "You ordered it."

"I thought it would be a little less gross."

"It's offal, onion, and oatmeal cooked in a sheep's stomach. The description on the menu didn't give you a clue?"

"Yeah, but it's Scotland's national dish—I figured it must have at least one redeeming feature."

"Perhaps if you tasted it..."

Sky poked at the lump with her fork and wrinkled her nose. "Or maybe I'll stick with the potatoes."

"Tatties."

"Whatever."

This year, Newcastle had been selected to host the New Dawn Film Festival, but one of the featured documentaries turned out to be a tad controversial, and death threats had left the organisers understandably twitchy. Blackwood, the security firm I co-owned along with my husband and two others, had been hired to provide security, and since this was a new, high-profile client, I'd flown to the UK with Sky to carry out additional checks before the event.

And from Newcastle, it had only been a short hop up to Edinburgh to make one last attempt to solve a cold case that had been bugging me for ages.

Seven-year-old Mila Carmody had disappeared five years ago, snatched from her bed in the middle of the night in every parent's worst nightmare. No witnesses, no ransom demands, and no sign of the little girl despite a manhunt involving half the cops in Virginia plus the FBI. The only physical clue had been a tiny speck of blood on the latch of Mila's window, a speck that didn't belong to her or anybody else in the various DNA databases the authorities maintained.

When the cops failed to find her kidnapper, Mila's wealthy family had hired us to do a case review. Then they'd fired us when we suggested a family member might have been involved. There'd been signs of an inside job—no evidence of a break-in, a lack of a struggle, and not one peep from the family's dog. But when we'd asked questions about Mila's uncle, her father—his brother—hadn't been impressed.

And now it seemed we might have been barking up the wrong tree entirely.

A trail of breadcrumbs had led us to Scotland, and if the genetic genealogist advising us was right, the owner of the blood speck found in Mila's bedroom had relatives living on the outskirts of Edinburgh. Our job this week was to collect a few DNA samples to see if she was right. Coffee cups, cigarette butts, used tissues... People tossed their DNA away every day. All we had to do was follow them around and pick it up. Blackwood's London forensics lab was on standby to process the samples, and in between waiting for results and strategising, we had time to kill. So far, Scotland was living up to my expectations—this afternoon, we'd climbed a bloody great hill in the rain because it was "scenic," and then we'd got stuck in a traffic jam caused by cows.

Oh, and Sky was absolutely right about the haggis—it was gross.

But I couldn't admit that.

"How are you gonna survive jungle training if you can't even eat pub food?"

"Do they have oatmeal in the jungle?"

"So you're saying it's the oatmeal that's the problem?"

"Shut up."

Hallie sat beside her, looking oh-so smug with her fish and chips. She'd tagged along because the Carmody file had landed on her desk several months ago, and she'd grown as curious about it as I had. Now she opened the guidebook.

"We could do a ghost tour tomorrow? Walk around the underground vaults and the graveyards?"

"What, you think we haven't seen enough dead people recently?"

Surprisingly, Hallie's body count was higher than mine for the past month. I'd been slacking.

"Okay, then how about a trip to Loch Ness?"

"How far is that?"

"The app says three and a half hours, so with you driving, it's around two hours away."

"A four-hour round trip to see a giant pond? The monster can rest easy. We still have samples to collect, and that'll take up most of tomorrow."

Not so long ago, I'd have said we didn't have time for any sightseeing at all, but I'd come to realise the importance of R&R. Ditto for my husband. A wake-up call involving a mental breakdown and a near-death experience respectively had led us to re-evaluate our priorities. Now we tried to spread the load and also take the occasional vacation, although those didn't always work out as intended.

"So, the ghost tour?" Hallie asked.

Which would be a waste of time. "Ghosts don't exist."

"How do you know?" Sky stole a forkful of my lasagne. "You snooze, you lose."

"Hey, eat your haggis." I moved my plate farther out of reach. "There's no evidence ghosts are real, and plenty of evidence of people faking them. Pretty sure the Loch Ness monster doesn't exist either."

"There are photos."

"And most of them have been discredited."

"*Most* of them."

"Okay, fine, we'll go on the 'ghost' tour. Happy now?"

Sky glanced at the mess on her plate. "Partially."

Out of curiosity, I forked up a piece of haggis. I'd once eaten a raw bat—albeit out of necessity rather than by choice —and lived to tell the tale, so I figured I could do this. Hmm. It wasn't quite as bad as I'd anticipated.

"Well?" Sky asked.

"If sausage and porridge had a love child and sprinkled it with pepper, this would be it. Did you ever go to that dodgy kebab place on Mile End Road?"

"Maybe."

"Then you've survived worse. Woman up and try the haggis."

"Or I could skip straight to dessert."

"That's against the—"

My phone rang, and Sky sat back, grinning. Dammit, what did Nick want?

"Did anyone ever tell you what an impeccable sense of timing you have?" I asked him.

Nick was a former Navy SEAL, an ex-lover, a current colleague, and one of my oldest friends. But like me, he rarely called someone to shoot the shit, which meant he had either a question or a problem.

"Are you still in Scotland? What did I interrupt?"

"Yes, and Sky's attempt to eat haggis."

"Sorry I missed that."

"Just don't mention it to Bradley, or we'll be having a ceilidh before you know it." My darling assistant would use any excuse for a party. If I blinked, my entire house would be covered in tartan. "And then we'll *all* be eating haggis."

An added bonus of treating the trip as a semi-vacation? If we wasted enough time, we'd miss the Thanksgiving nightmare Bradley had planned for next week.

"Does haggis really taste that bad? Bet we've both eaten worse in the jungle."

"You'd also have to wear a kilt."

"Right."

"And, as tradition dictates, no underwear."

"Guess I'll keep quiet about the haggis," Nick said.

"Glad we're on the same page."

"How's the DNA collecting going?"

"Two samples down, four more to go at this stage. But you didn't call to discuss haggis and DNA, did you?"

"I need a favour."

See? "What sort of favour?"

"Kind of a... I guess you could call it a welfare check."

"On who?"

"You remember Fletcher?"

"Your half-brother?" Who could forget him? He was a younger, cuter version of Nick, except because his father wasn't a callous arsehole the way Nick's had been, Fletcher hadn't built up the same hard shields. His sweetness ran closer to the surface. "Isn't he counting puffins in the Arctic?"

"The Antarctic, and it's penguins, not puffins."

"Tell me you don't want me to take a trip to the Antarctic."

Antarctica was thousands of bloody miles away, and I hadn't set foot there in years. I was far closer to the Arctic. A quick hop over to Iceland or Norway...

"No, Glendoon."

"Glen-what?"

"The map suggests it's roughly an hour north-west of Edinburgh."

I was lost. The waitress came back and began clearing away the remains of Sky's haggis, which was something of a disappointment because she still hadn't taken a bite, but I conjured up a smile and pointed at the sticky toffee pudding on the dessert menu. If Nick was about to ruin my evening, I at least wanted cake first.

"You're gonna have to start at the beginning. What does this have to do with Fletcher?"

"Last year, he spent the summer in Thailand, volunteering at a turtle sanctuary, and he got to know a girl there. Not in *that* way—she had a boyfriend, and Fletch wouldn't muscle in —but they stayed in touch."

"She's Scottish?"

"No, the boyfriend was Scottish. Paige—that's the girl—is from Wyoming, but she was studying at Berkeley."

"Still not seeing how this gets us to Glendoon? Is it the girl that you want me to check up on? Paige?"

"Fletch is worried about her. They emailed back and forth for months, and then suddenly...nothing. He figured she was just busy moving—she'd planned to study abroad for a year at Edinburgh University—but after a bunch of emails went unanswered, he called me for advice. So I suggested sending one last message asking her for a single sentence if she was okay, the same if she wanted him to leave her alone. If he didn't get a response, then I'd dig into things."

Hallie had obviously been eavesdropping because she slid her tablet in my direction. According to the website she'd found, Glendoon—population 357 humans and twice that many cows–was famous for its whisky distillery, for hosting the local cheese festival, and for spawning the runner-up in the caber toss at last year's Highland Games. Place sounded like a riot.

"Paige replied?" I asked Nick.

"She called. In tears. She split with the boyfriend right after they bought a house together, and now she's stuck in Scotland."

Ah. "In Glendoon?"

"Right."

"And how the hell did she end up buying a house in Glendoon?"

"By accident. Fletch got that much, but then the call cut off, and now she's not answering her phone. His research project wrapped up last week, but a storm's stopping him from flying out himself right now."

"So you want me to make sure she's still breathing?"

"I'll buy you lunch if you do."

"Not haggis."

"Anything but haggis," Nick confirmed.

"And you'll wear a kilt?"

"You know what? I'll just head to the airport myself."

I sighed. I wasn't about to let a damsel stay in distress, and Nick knew it. "Fine, I'll go. Got an address?"

"Like a house number and a zip code?"

"Postcode in Scotland, and that's generally what an address consists of."

"So that's a negative, but the place is half-derelict and—I quote—creepy as all get out."

Fantastic. "Lunch just became dinner. Three courses and wine."

Nick blew me a kiss. "Babe, I'll even throw in a bottle of good Scotch."

If I'd known what we were about to get into, I'd have bought my own damn Scotch, poured it down my throat, and then hit myself over the head with the empty bottle. My husband always joked that trouble followed me around, and I was beginning to think he might be right.

2

EMMY

"Hey, it looks as if we're going on the ghost tour a day early," Hallie said from the back seat. "Actually, it might be more of a monster tour."

Precisely what I didn't need to hear at nine p.m. while driving through the Scottish countryside in the dark. The rolling hills had been quite pretty when we made the journey in daylight two days ago, but at night when we were the only vehicle on the road for miles, the overhanging trees and long shadows made the landscape eerie as fuck.

An owl came out of nowhere, a winged wraith that buzzed the car before disappearing into the gloom again. A combination of experience and willpower meant I didn't show any outward signs of my surprise, but my heart skipped half a beat as the bird nearly plastered itself across the windscreen.

"Monsters? Dare I ask?"

"According to local legend, the forest around Glendoon is home to a beast that's half eagle, half wolf."

Thanks, Nick. He'd conveniently forgotten to mention that part, and I didn't even have a gun with me.

"Which half is which?" Sky asked. "Like, is it an eagle with a wolf's head? Or a giant dog with a beak?"

"Uh, so I think it's a wolf with wings. And talons. Oh, and its eyes glow red."

"So basically a flying nightmare, then?"

"Yeah, that's exactly it. Wait, this article says it also has a snake for a tail."

"What kind of snake? A poisonous one? Or the sort that squeezes you to death?"

Good grief. "Guys, it's not real. I bet the local tourist board made it up to boost visitor numbers."

Because who would want to go to a cheese festival? I mean, I liked cheese, don't get me wrong, but if I was going to devote a day to eating it, I'd do that in France with a good bottle of red and slightly more sunshine. A pool, a lounge chair, my husband at my side...

"Reports go back as far as the seventeenth century. Was tourism a thing back then?"

"The villagers probably borrowed an old story to add a layer of authenticity. Check out the gift shop—if they're selling little clay models of the Glendoon Monster, then you know they did it for the money."

Sky fiddled with the radio until she found a station playing old rock songs. Soon, Bryan Adams was belting out of the speakers, and I calculated we had six more tracks until we arrived at Paige's "creepy as all get out" home. In the end, it hadn't been that hard to find. We'd just taken a look at one of those "How much is my property worth?" websites and zeroed in on Glendoon. Only five properties had sold nearby in the past year, and of those, two were flats, one was a rather nice detached farmhouse with equestrian facilities, and a fourth included a small shopfront that had formerly been the village post office. The fifth had been purchased at auction four months ago, and the picture painted by the now-archived online catalogue was, in a word, grim. Glendoon Hall was crumbling on its foundations. And those foundations probably had subsidence. No wonder Paige had been in tears if that was where she was living.

The darkness wrapped around us as we drove down ever-narrower lanes. Three miles to go, two, one...

"Reckon that's the place?" Sky asked.

There was no handy sign to confirm, but there didn't seem to be any other properties around. And the iron gates hanging askew from ivy-covered pillars were open—practically an invitation. I nosed the SUV into the pitted driveway, slowly because some of the potholes deserved postcodes in their own right.

The house soon came into view, looming out of the trees beneath a clouded moon. Upon first glance, the place looked deserted—there wasn't a single light on, and the only sound was the rustle of trees—but a closer inspection showed signs of life. The tarpaulins tacked over broken windows were clean, and footprints near the front door had been left since the earlier rainstorm. I tried knocking.

No answer, but I hadn't been expecting one. The cobwebs around the door told me it hadn't been opened in a long while. Hallie's gaze strayed towards the surrounding forest, and she shivered. From the cold or from unease? Probably both.

"You think Paige is out?" she asked.

"If this was my home, then I would be."

Sky knocked again. "Maybe the monster got her?"

Oh, for crying out loud, she actually sounded serious. "The only monsters on this earth are humans."

Fresh tyre tracks in the dirt led around the side of the building, and I followed them with Sky and Hallie bringing up the rear. Fuck, I'd always thought that Riverley Hall—the gothic monstrosity I shared with my husband in Virginia—was creepy, but this place was on a whole other level.

Okay, there was a car, a small red hatchback parked in the courtyard of an old stable block, the horses long gone, the top and bottom loose-box doors closed up. But where was the driver?

"Hello?" I called, and it was like shouting into the void. "Is anyone there?"

Nothing.

"Should we go back to the hotel?" Hallie asked.

"We can't. This is a welfare check. If there's anybody here, we have to find them."

And Paige's call with Fletcher had cut out suddenly. I didn't believe for a moment that she'd stumbled across an eagle-wolf hybrid, whatever local lore said, but falling through a rotten floor in this place was a very real possibility. What if she was lying somewhere with a broken leg?

"You mean...go in *there*?" Hallie lifted her chin towards the main house.

"If necessary. We can look through the windows first."

"Most of them are covered up."

"Then let's check the ones that aren't. If you and Sky take the north side, then—"

"You mean split up?"

"It'll be faster."

"What about safety in numbers?"

"We all—" I'd been about to say that we all knew how to handle ourselves, but Hallie hadn't had the easiest of times over the past month, so I relented. "Okay, we can go together."

Or not.

The back door was secured by a hasp and padlock attached to the outside, and when we headed for the north of the house, a bramble thicket blocked our way. Unless somebody had lifted a tarpaulin and climbed through a window—

unlikely when there was a door available—there was nobody in the main house. Which left the outbuildings.

"Let's go back to the stable block. That's where the car is."

And I'd also spotted a Portaloo tucked into a corner beside the rusting remains of a tractor and a forest of weeds. I'd assumed it was there for contractors to use, but what if it was there for Paige? She wouldn't be far away. Nobody wanted to walk half a mile if they needed to pee at midnight.

"Paige!" I yelled, making Hallie jump. Oops. "Are you there? My name is Emmy, and I work for Blackwood Security. We've just come to check you're okay. Fletcher sent us."

A long moment passed. I was about to yell again when one of the stable doors opened a crack and a pale face peered through the gap.

"Paige?"

She gave the briefest of nods. "Did Fletcher really ask you to come?"

"He's very worried. Are you all right?"

Her answer came in the form of tears. Aw, hell. Sky looked at me, and I looked at Sky, and then Hallie pushed past both of us. Thank fuck.

"Hey, it's okay. Are you here on your own?"

"Y-y-yes."

"What happened earlier? Fletcher said your call cut out?"

"My phone battery died. I should've realised it was going to, but I wasn't thinking straight, and..." Paige wiped her eyes with a sleeve. "This is all such a mess."

"You couldn't recharge the battery?"

"The generator won't start. I can charge the phone tomorrow at college, and my laptop, but tonight..."

"You don't have a car charger?"

"A mouse ate it. I don't even know how it got into the freaking car." She shrugged, helpless. "How do you know Fletcher?"

"We work with his brother."

"Nick? His brother's called Nick, right?"

"Yes, Nick Goldman. He's still in the US, but he asked us to come and check you were okay."

I peered past Paige into the old stable. A folding cot was positioned against one wall, a couple of camping chairs sat on either side of a table, and one corner had been set up as a cooking area. A stack of bottled water towered over a portable hotplate, and the only light came from a row of candles on a shelf. She was living in there? In freaking November?

"Forgive my bluntness here, but what the actual fuck?" Paige blanched a little, and yeah, I should have phrased that better, but it was ten p.m. and cold and dark and we'd just driven an hour across Scotland. "How long have you been camping in a stable?"

"Nearly three months."

"I suppose the more appropriate question is why?"

"It all went wrong. *Everything.*"

"Could you elaborate?"

Hallie wrapped an arm around her shoulders. "Why don't we sit in...there?"

She helped Paige into one of the chairs, and I motioned Hallie to take the other. In the flickering light, I got a better look at the girl Fletcher Braun cared for enough to ask Nick to pull strings. A dainty blonde waif with big blue wide-set eyes and an elfin jaw, pretty but tired. Worn around the edges. And she gave off a vibe that might have been innocent or naive, depending on the situation. Yeah, people would take advantage of Paige, and she probably wouldn't even realise they were doing it. Tiny silver stars sparkled in her ears as a draft blew across the candles, and she wrapped her arms around herself as we stared at her. She didn't like being the centre of attention. An introvert?

Sky perched on the edge of the cot while I mooched

around the place. Plastic boxes contained textbooks and novels and clothes and a hell of a lot of ramen, and a fan heater sat silently beside them. Buckets had been positioned at strategic intervals, presumably to catch incoming water. Sheesh. No electricity meant no heat, and according to the weather forecast, it was meant to freeze tonight. She couldn't stay here, not like this.

"How about you start from the beginning?"

Sky gave me a "this is gonna be good" look. We'd both grown up on the streets of London, and neither of us was a stranger to homelessness—I'd spent two years living in a storage closet, and she'd been squatting in a former pub when we first met—but winding up in a stable in Bumfuck, Scotland with no power in the middle of winter was...special.

"The beginning?" Paige gave a nervous laugh. "So I was dating this guy..."

3

EMMY

"There's *always* a guy involved," Hallie muttered, and granted, she hadn't had the best of luck with men until the most recent one, but Paige needed to tell her story. I put a finger to my lips.

"Go on."

"We met two years ago when we were both at Berkeley," Paige said. "It was my first year of college, and Jez was on an exchange study program during his third, and we ended up living next door to each other. Then we started dating. I thought he was the *one*, you know?"

"So, what went wrong?"

"Well, he had to finish his degree in Edinburgh, so we went long-distance, and I missed him so, so much. We'd been together that whole year, and then he was just...gone. The loss, it felt almost like grief. A piece of my heart was on the other side of the ocean, and even though we called each other every day, it wasn't enough. It felt as if we were growing apart, and FaceTime couldn't fix it. So I applied to study abroad for a year myself, even though I wasn't totally sure how I'd afford it."

"In Edinburgh?"

"Yes, in Edinburgh." She bobbed her head. "And I swear I've never been so happy as when I got accepted. But not two days later, my Grandma Charlotte passed away. That's my grandma on my pop's side, and we were close but not *super* close because my mom and dad got divorced when I was six, and I spent more time with my mom. But Grandma Charlotte died, and it was still real sad because she'd always been kind to me."

I was beginning to wish I'd asked her to start the story halfway through. Paige didn't half waffle. "I'm sorry for your loss."

"Aw, that's so kind of you. Anyhow, I flew home to Wyoming for the burial, and I thought it would be real sombre, but she'd asked everyone to wear pink because it was her favourite colour, you know? So I wore a pink dress, one I bought in the sale at TJ Maxx, but it was real pretty, and she'd picked out the music herself, not hymns, but 'Over the Rainbow' and 'Wind Beneath My Wings' and 'What a Wonderful World,' happy songs, but that only made me feel the loss harder. Why does it hurt more to remember the good times?"

Did she expect an answer? Apparently not, because after a few more sniffles, she carried on.

"And while I was there, Pop told me that Grandma Charlotte had left me some money in her will. Which turned out to be quite a lot of money because I was her only grandchild, and it felt like fate, you know? That I could use her gift to follow my dream of coming to Scotland."

Okay, now we were getting closer. "And you used the money to buy this place?"

"How did you know?"

"A lucky guess."

"Jez said it would be such a waste to rent when I had cash

sitting in the bank. That we'd just be lining the landlord's pockets, and wouldn't it be better if we could keep the money for ourselves? For our future? So he had the idea of buying an apartment, one that needed sprucing up, and we could live in it for a year and then sell the place for a profit when I went back to California to finish my degree. Jez has a job now, and he said he'd pay for the materials we needed—the paint and stuff—and he'd help with the work. We were meant to get m-m-married, and he was gonna come to the US with me while I finished my degree, and then we thought we'd travel for a while until we decided where to live permanently."

"Stating the obvious, this isn't an apartment?"

"But it was meant to be!" Another tear rolled down Paige's cheek, and Hallie found a tissue from somewhere. "Jez said the best place to pick up a project home was in an auction, and we found the perfect property in Edinburgh. A two-bedroom apartment that needed a better kitchen, fresh tiles in the bathroom, new carpets, and a coat of paint. Lot twenty-seven. The catalogue said it was lot twenty-seven, and I had to do the bidding because Jez was in a meeting he couldn't skip, but I didn't realise they'd added more properties into the list, and the auctioneer, his accent was so...so *Scottish*, and he talked so fast, so I bid on lot twenty-seven and this"—she gestured towards the door—"was what I got."

Sky gave a low whistle. "You couldn't just have cancelled?"

"They said that when I bid, I entered into a legally binding contract. The seller threatened to sue me for fraud if I pulled out, plus they'd have kept the deposit anyway, and that was ten percent. The auction guy emailed me some pictures, and I guess they must've been taken a while ago because it honestly didn't look this bad." A hysterical giggle burst from Paige's throat. "I was even excited. I mean, it's a big house, and the village is so pretty. And it was only for a year. Sure, Edinburgh's an hour away, but I thought we could commute."

"Jez didn't feel the same way?"

"He came to visit the place, and then he called and said it was awful, and he hadn't signed up for this. He broke up with me *over the freaking phone* two days before I was due to fly here. And...and I didn't know what to do. I mean, what *could* I do? It was too late to switch my studies back to California, and I had nowhere else to live."

"Staying with a parent wasn't an option?"

"I considered that, but my mom was so excited for me, and I guess...I guess I didn't want to let her down. She thinks I'm having a great time here." Paige choked out a laugh. "When I send photos, I'm real careful to edit them first."

"What about your dad?"

"He remarried three years ago, and my stepmom and I, we don't get along. Grandma Charlotte didn't like her either, which is why she left the money to me instead of Pop, and he wasn't happy about that."

Well, Paige was right about one thing. This *was* a mess. A mess of epic proportions. The question was, what the hell was I meant to do about it? We could hardly take off and leave the girl here on her own. Did she even have running water?

"Why don't you sell the place?" Hallie asked. "Then you could buy an apartment instead."

"You think I didn't try that?" Paige's voice headed towards hysterical. "It's been on the market since the day I moved in, plus I listed in two auctions and it didn't meet the reserve. Nobody wants to buy it, seeing as it's falling down *and* haunted."

"Haunted? Ha!" Sky grinned. "I knew it. Is there an actual ghost? Or just the monster in the woods?"

"Both, but it's the Beast that everyone's scared of."

For the love of fuck. "There's no ghost, and there's no monster, beast, or anything else."

"I've h-h-heard it. And seen it."

"The Beast?"

"Y-y-yes."

"And what did it look like?"

"I only saw its eyes, but they were watching me. And the way it howls…"

"It was probably a fox. They sound freaky at night."

"The eyes were red."

"Fox eyes can reflect red if you shine a flashlight on them. So can owl eyes."

And alligator eyes. I'd found that out while canoeing across a river one sweltering night in Louisiana when I'd turned on my torch and a dozen fiery orbs looked back at me. Fuck, I'd never paddled so fast in my life.

"But I didn't have a flashlight. They were just there in the dark, staring at me."

"So there was another light source. The moon, perhaps."

"It was cloudy."

Okay, that was slightly weird, but I found it easier to believe in the existence of a sliver of moonlight than a cryptid.

"What about the ghost?" Sky asked. "Have you seen the ghost?"

"No, but groans come from the house at night. I won't go in there after dark. And not much in daylight, either. There are holes in the floors, and the roof leaks all over."

Bloody hell. Right now, I wasn't sure whether Paige was dumb as a box of rocks for ending up in this situation or just incredibly unlucky. I checked my watch. Time was ticking on, and I didn't fancy hanging around here until the early hours to find out the answer.

"Pack up whatever you need for tomorrow, and we'll take you to a hotel for tonight."

"But I don't have any spare money, not a cent."

"I'll pay for the room. You're not staying here."

"I..." Paige bit her lip. "But I don't even know you."

"So borrow my phone and call Fletcher. You know *him*, and a fiver says he won't want you staying here either."

She stared at the phone in my hand, then finally shook her head. "I can't."

"You don't want him to know how bad things are?"

Her watery eyes told me I'd hit the nail on the head. She was embarrassed. And the reason she was embarrassed was that she cared what he thought. Paige liked Fletcher, and from reading between the lines during my conversation with Nick, I figured Fletcher felt the same way. Awww.

"He must think I'm such a dumbass."

A reasonable assumption, although I didn't say that. No, for once I managed to dredge up a modicum of tact.

"I'm sure that's not true. Come on, let's get you packed, and then we can find somewhere warm. Have you eaten a proper dinner?"

"The stove wouldn't work either."

"Then we'll order food too." Sky would probably be thrilled about that. "Find a bag, and bring what you need for college next week."

"You don't just owe me a bottle of Scotch, you owe me a whole damn distillery."

On screen, Nick sucked in a breath. I could see from the background that he'd made it home, but he'd attended a client meeting this afternoon, a briefing with an up-and-coming pop star who'd been targeted by a stalker. Her manager had insisted on extra security for her world tour, which took a reasonable amount of coordination by Nick's team. And I suspected the meeting had overrun because he hadn't had a chance to change out of his dress shirt yet.

"How bad is it?" he asked.

"Physically, Paige is in one piece. Mentally and financially, she's screwed." I gave him a brief precis of the situation. "We got her a hotel room on the next floor down for tonight, but obviously that's not a long-term solution."

"What if I covered the cost of an apartment for the rest of the school year?"

"That'd still only solve part of the problem. Her money's tied up in a ruin."

"Is it salvageable?"

"How would I know? One, I'm not an architect, and two, I only saw the place in the dark."

"Can you take another look tomorrow? Maybe I could hire a builder to help out?" Nick ran a hand through his dark hair. "I need to talk with Fletch."

"Does he just like her? Or does he *like* her?"

"The second one. At least, I think so. But he also swore off girls after he split with Sarah, so who can say?"

"What happened with Sarah, anyway?"

Nick reached for a glass of something. Whisky, judging by the colour of it, which meant he wasn't happy either. He only drank hard liquor when he was stressed.

"She fucked one of their professors, and Fletch found out. But you didn't hear that from me, okay?"

"Understood. That had to sting."

"Yeah, he was real cut up about it, but at least she showed her true colours before they got a place together."

"Every cloud, silver lining, blah blah blah. You gonna call Fletcher tonight?"

"Assuming the storm hasn't taken the comms out."

"I'll need a sitrep in the morning."

"You'll have it." Nick's voice softened, and he held out a hand towards the screen. "Thanks for stepping in, babe."

Even though I was very much in love with Black now, even though it had been over a decade since Nick and I were together, that smile still made my heart skip.

"Anytime, Nicky. Anytime."

4

HALLIE

"Black told me that trouble follows Emmy around, and he was totally right."

Ford's forehead creased into a frown. "Is this the type of trouble that's likely to put you in danger again?"

A part of me hated to worry him, but at the same time, warmth spread through me because *he was worried*. I'd never been in a proper relationship before, not one where a man cared enough to call each night I was away and ended every conversation with "I love you." Ford was the man I hadn't known I needed, and now he was the man I never wanted to live without.

"Only if I fall through a rotten floor."

"What kind of dive are you staying in? I always figured Emmy would be a five-star gal."

"Oh, the hotel's amazing. My room has a view of Edinburgh Castle, and the bathroom's bigger than the trailer I grew up in. Take a look."

I showed him around the bathroom, panning across the fancy robe and slippers and the basket of luxury toiletries. Housekeeping had left chocolates on my pillow, and a small cupboard held tea, coffee, and packages of cookies, none of which I could eat, seeing as I'd stuffed myself with two dinners tonight. Technically, the hotel restaurant had been closed when we arrived back at nearly midnight, but Emmy had asked the concierge nicely, and a chef had served us pizza in a private dining room.

"I'm impressed."

"It's dark outside, but I can show you the castle in the morning." Duh, I couldn't. Hello, time zones. "Actually, you'll still be asleep, but I can take a picture."

"Early start tomorrow?"

"I'm meeting an investigator from Blackwood's Edinburgh office at eight."

"I thought you were working with Emmy and Sky on this?"

"I was." And Ford hadn't exactly been enthusiastic about the prospect, mainly because he was a cop and Emmy and Sky tended to pay lip service to the law when it suited them. "But they got pulled onto a side project."

Ford's sigh was more resigned than anything else. He didn't like the fact that Emmy bent the rules, but he tolerated her habits better than I'd ever thought he would, probably because they had the same goal at heart. They both wanted justice. It was merely their methodology that differed.

"Do I want to know about the side project?"

"It's not a case. It's barely anything to do with Blackwood at all." Ford sipped from a bottle of beer as I summarised tonight's Highland adventure. When I was in Richmond, he spent most of his time at my apartment, but tonight, he was back on his boat a little way down the James River. "So Nick asked Emmy to go back in daylight and see just how bad of a shape the place is in. I think that maybe he'll hire an electrician or something to help Paige out, seeing as she's a friend of his brother."

"She's really living in a stable?"

"I'd hardly call it living. Existing, more like."

"Just be careful—there's a reason derelict buildings usually have warning signs."

"I will, I swear. Nothing's going to happen." Okay, I might have left out the story of the monster, but I was inclined to side with Emmy on that one—it didn't exist. At least, I hoped not. "I'm not even planning to go inside."

"Good. Leave that to the experts. Any news on your DNA samples yet?"

"We couriered the first two down to the lab, and they're being processed. But we'd like to collect four more."

The Carmody file was sitting on Ford's desk as well as on my own. And since Blackwood no longer even worked for the Carmody family and we were only in Scotland due to Emmy's sheer bloody-mindedness and my ambition to see the case finally closed, the investigation was technically Ford's responsibility. If we got a lead, we could pass it on as an "anonymous tip."

Mila had been a child when she disappeared, an innocent little girl. Her truth needed to be told. Statistics said she'd died long ago, but after the events of the past month, I'd never stop believing that there was a chance, just the tiniest chance, that she was still breathing. And if she was alive, I wanted to find her.

Once again, Ford wasn't entirely on board with Blackwood's methods, but he wasn't trying to stop us either.

"Then I suppose I should wish you luck," he said.

"I miss you."

"Ditto. And Mercy said to say 'hola.'"

"You spoke with Mercy?"

Mercy was my roommate, and she was usually shy around people, especially men. And with good reason. But over the past six months, she'd gradually started coming out of her shell.

"She called to say that Cora's grandma made empanadas, and did I want some?"

"Marisol's empanadas are the best."

"Can't disagree there. Mercy also said that when I moved in, I'd have to get used to eating them all the time because Marisol never stops cooking."

"Oh my gosh, that's so true. You'll have to try her bandeja paisa, but don't plan on doing anything energetic for at least three hours afterward."

"Plum, do you know anything about the 'moving in' part?"

"Uh..." My brain finally caught up with my mouth and... I was busted. "Uh, so we might have discussed it."

"Me moving in with the two of you?"

"Yes? I mean, we were talking about the boat and how you can't sail it properly because it's so far up the river, so Mercy asked why you didn't move it closer to the sea, and I explained that your commute would be too long since the boat's also your home, and she suggested that you just move in with us officially since you spend half of your time in our apartment anyway. But I'll totally understand if you hate that idea, because we've only been together for a short time, and this is all so new for both of us, and—"

"Mercy would be okay with me moving in?"

"It was her idea."

"Sometimes people say things they don't mean."

"No, she's really fine with it."

"And what about you? How do you feel?"

About sharing my home with the man I loved? About falling asleep next to him every night and waking up in his arms each morning? About talking over the mundanities of my day and having a sounding board when I was stressed?

About spending lazy weekends in bed and then being late for work on Monday mornings because Ford decided to get dirty in the shower?

"Giving up half of my closet space will be hard, but I think I can cope."

"Guess I'd better start looking at marinas in Virginia Beach, then."

My chest tightened. Were we really doing this? "You'll move in?"

"Won't be tomorrow, but soon."

Wow. The most significant decision of my life, maybe Ford's too, and we'd made it from opposite sides of the world.

"I really wish I could kiss you right now."

"How do you feel about phone sex?"

Six months ago, I'd have hung up in horror, but now? With Ford?

"I'll try anything once."

Blackwood's Edinburgh location was a fraction of the size of headquarters, more like the satellite office in Richmond I worked out of occasionally, but old rather than modern. It looked as if someone had taken three townhouses and knocked them together. Inside, the receptionist showed me up to a small meeting room on the third floor and told me Alasdair would be with me shortly.

"Coffee?" she offered.

"Do you have espresso?"

"Of course. Single shot or double?"

"Double."

It had been a late night. Turned out that phone sex was one of my new favourite things. Ford scored an A-plus in dirty talk, filthy little instructions whispered across an ocean that turned my insides to liquid silk. My cheeks heated from the memory—awkward when I was just about to meet a colleague. I forced myself to walk to the window, to focus on the view of the street below and think about anything but Ford.

The office overlooked a square, a green oasis in the heart of the city. People scurried past under an inky sky, wrapped up in coats and gloves and scarves. But the icy wind showed no mercy. I'd felt its bite as I speed-walked over from the hotel, too cold to slow down and enjoy the scenery. I didn't envy Emmy and Sky on their trip to Glendoon.

"Hallie Chastain?"

Yes, I was taken now, but I couldn't deny the Scottish accent was incredibly hot. The guy in the doorway held a drink in each hand, my tiny espresso and an oversized mug with *I'm too sexy for my kilt* written across it. I didn't doubt that claim for a moment.

"That's right."

He set the cups down on the table and held out a hand. "Dair McLeod."

My freaking palms were sweating. His grip was firm but not too firm, and when he smiled, my reflex reaction was to grin like an idiot.

"Thanks for agreeing to help today."

"Just doing my job. The big boss said we're collecting DNA samples?"

"Yes, from four people, possibly more depending on what they show. We've already done two."

I fumbled my tablet out of my purse and dropped it. Dair bent to pick it up at the same time I did, and we came within a hair's breadth of cracking heads before I lost my balance and fell on my ass.

Way to make an impression, Hallie.

Worse, the wall of the meeting room was made from glass,

and despite it being a Saturday, there were still a few people working in the open-plan office beyond. Every single one of them turned to stare. Emmy had said that this trip would be a great way to start building my network overseas, and now the entire Edinburgh office thought I was a klutz. Terrific.

Dair had my tablet in one hand, and he held out the other to help me up. His smile reminded me of Nick's, but his hair was lighter, more of a dirty blond, and although he wasn't old —early thirties, at a guess—he had creases around his eyes. From the sun or from laughter? Probably the latter if the weather here was anything to go by.

"Thanks."

"Screen's still in one piece." A small blessing. "So, what's the plan?"

The plan... The plan... Right, *the plan*.

"Uh, so we have four clusters to target. Did Emmy explain what we're doing?"

"She said you'd brief me."

Which felt weird because Dair had way more experience at this job than I did, but if Emmy had confidence in me, then I couldn't let her down. Or Mila Carmody. Wherever she was, she was counting on me too.

"Five years ago, a little girl disappeared from her bedroom during the night."

"In Scotland?"

"No, in Richmond, Virginia. And the only clue we've never been able to run down is a speck of blood that was found on her window latch. The offender doesn't have a profile in the system, but a genetic genealogist recently reviewed the file as part of another case, and she thinks he has Scottish roots."

"Another case? He did it again?"

"We thought for a while that he might have, and there's still a slim chance, but we're inclined to believe not." I shrugged. "Which leaves us here. Valerie—that's our genealogist—believes a guy called Bobby Miller is a second cousin of the man we're looking for. He lives in Bathgate—do you know it?"

"Aye, I've got a cousin who lives there."

Small world. "Valerie began building a family tree around Bobby, using the information we have available, and she's identified six possible branches. So we need to obtain a DNA sample from each branch and see which, if any, gets us closer to our suspect."

"And you say you've collected two samples already?"

"Yesterday. They're on their way to London for processing."

"What's your timescale for acquiring the remaining four?"

"ASAP. Emmy can't stay in Scotland for long."

"She's still here? Figured she'd gone already, seeing as I've been asked to step in."

"There was a small problem last night, and she's had to drive to Glendoon today."

"Glendoon? Och, she's not gone chasing after the Beast, has she?"

"You've heard of it?"

"Aye, it's well known in these parts. Head of a wolf, wings of an eagle, and a wee snake on its arse. A modern-day Chimera."

"A what?"

"Chimera. You're not big on Greek mythology?"

"I must've skipped that class."

Dair gave a hearty laugh. "Always bunked off Friday-morning German lessons myself. Rugby practice was on a Thursday evening, and we used to like a wee dram or three afterwards. The Chimera was a fire-breathing monster with the head of a lion, the head and body of a goat, and a serpent for a tail."

"He had two heads?"

"*She* had two heads. Three if you count the snake at the rear."

I suppressed a shudder. "But it's not real, right?"

"The Chimera or the Beast of Glendoon?"

"Well, both?"

"Can't judge when it comes to the Chimera, but there's something in the forest at Glendoon. Locals hear it howling, and one or two of them have found its tracks in the forest."

"I saw a picture of one of the footprints online, but it looked like a dog paw to me."

"Naw, it's bigger than a dog. And my cousin Hamish swears he saw it once."

"What exactly did he see?"

"He was hiking with a friend in the forest beyond Glendoon, and a shadow crossed the path in front of them. Knowing Hamish, he was probably pissed as a fart himself, but he swears he didn't imagine the thing. But he did fall over a tree root running to his car, and we had to take him to A&E for X-rays."

"Was he hurt?"

"Broken ankle. Six weeks in a cast."

Ouch.

"I definitely drew the long straw today." Although Emmy and Sky versus the Beast of Glendoon would be an interesting fight to watch. "When you say bigger than a dog, how big are we talking?"

"Anywhere between six feet and ten feet tall, depending on which story you believe."

"Ten feet tall? Does it walk on its hind legs?"

"Like one of those Egyptian gods? Again, that depends on who's telling the story. Hamish said it ran on all fours."

"Maybe I should warn Emmy..."

"If the stories I've heard about *her* are anywhere near true, it's the Beast who should be quaking in its boots. Now, where's this list of clusters?"

I set my tablet on the table and took a seat. This visit to Scotland was turning into more of an adventure than I'd planned.

5

EMMY

In daylight, Glendoon Hall looked both better and worse.

Once, it had been a grand old building, and when I said "building," I meant "castle." It had a fucking turret at each corner and battlements running along the roofline. Patches of the beige sandstone were still visible under a layer of grime, and a square tower rose in the middle. The place had character in spades, but unfortunately, it also had holes in the roof, more broken windows than I could count, and—if the plump brown rat that appeared from under a window-tarpaulin and sauntered across the yard was any indication—a serious rodent infestation.

Sky pulled a face. "Nice."

"The rats come out more at night," Paige said. "I tried catching them, but they just kept coming back."

Kept coming back? "You mean you're catching them and then…letting them go?"

Paige pointed towards the trees behind the house. "Yes, right over there. I bought one of those humane traps and baited it with peanut butter."

Good grief.

Sky snorted but tried to turn it into a cough. "You need to take them miles away if you want to try that trick, and they'll still breed faster than you can relocate them."

Paige shuffled along behind us, hesitant, and I couldn't blame her. She'd been living a nightmare for the past three months. In the car yesterday, she'd crashed into sleep barely two miles from Glendoon, no doubt with relief that she didn't have to spend another night alone in the stable. I'd let her be because I knew exactly how that felt. More than once, I'd come home from an operation, running on empty, then slept for two days straight after I crawled into my own bed.

She'd woken briefly to eat dinner, paused for long enough between bites to tell us the place had no utilities connected. No water, no electricity, no gas, no landline. The girl had been in survival mode for a quarter of a year in between attending lectures and trying to get her coursework done. I understood how hard that was. So did Sky because we'd both been there. Now it was time to pay it forward.

Somehow.

Nick had called this morning—the middle of the night for him—to tell me the storm had passed over and Fletcher was waiting for a flight to Tierra del Fuego. Luckily, it was summer in the Antarctic, although I used the term "summer" loosely, or he'd have been stuck there for months in perpetual darkness. And yeah, Nick had been right about Fletcher's feelings for Paige. He'd been ready to empty his savings account to help her because, like Nick, he had a big heart, but Fletcher wasn't rich. If he spent everything he had, it might cover getting the electrical supply hooked up.

No, Nick was the rich one.

And he'd worked hard for his money, even the millions he'd inherited.

Nick and Fletcher... They had a complicated history, and it wasn't through any fault of their own. Nick's parents had divorced when he was ten, and he'd been shuttled back and forth between his arsehole of a father, a needy mother with terrible taste in men, and boarding schools—half a dozen of them because he'd had an unfortunate habit of getting expelled—until he hit eighteen.

From the age of twelve, he'd spent most of his vacations with Nicholas Goldman senior, being trained to take over his investment business. And also abused. Not physically, and he shied away from admitting the extent of it, even to himself, but that's what it was. Abuse. His father had manipulated him. If Nick wanted to eat, he'd had to earn the food by trading penny shares. Oh, he didn't need to cash them in—for his father, it was about the principle, not the money. If Nick made a profit, Daddy bought him steak. A loss got him peanut butter sandwiches. When Nick grew older, he'd rebelled against his father by stealing from the local grocery store, but either he hadn't been as proficient at subterfuge back then or getting caught had been a cry for help. I had no idea which— he didn't talk about it. Anyhow, his father had sent him to the toughest boarding school in Switzerland as a punishment, and Nick had excelled there. The discipline suited him.

Oh, and he was one hell of a skier.

Fast-forward twenty years... Nick knew more about balance sheets than he knew about guns, and as a former Navy SEAL, he knew a *lot* about guns. He also hated both financial statements and peanut butter with a passion. Sure, he still invested in projects that interested him as a sideline, and he could make money in his damn sleep, but he'd rather stick pins in his dick than discuss the stock market.

Fletcher, on the other hand, had been born after Nick's mom finally, finally met a man who didn't treat her like shit. A veterinarian. She'd worked as his admin assistant, then ended up marrying him, and Fletcher had grown up in a stable home. Loved. Perhaps even a little spoiled. Nick would always resent his mother for the way she'd treated him, *abandoned* him, but he got on okay with his half-brother. Looked out for him.

And by virtue of my friendship with Nick, that meant I had to look out for Paige.

"Did you have a builder check over the place?" I asked her.

"Not really."

"Not really?"

"I can't afford to get any work done on the house, but a guy from Glendoon village put some tiles back on the stable roof."

"Did you speak to a plumber? An electrician?"

"The electrician said the whole place needs to be rewired, and the plumber couldn't find the stopcock."

"How hard did he look?"

"Uh, not very hard? He didn't really want to come at all on account of the Beast living in the forest. Then when he got here, his foot went through the floor, and he said it was too dangerous to go poking around inside."

"What about an external stopcock? Is there one of those?"

I didn't know a huge amount about plumbing, but I had a rough idea of how houses worked. Why? Because if I knew how they were put together, then it was easier for me to take them apart. Every time I went into a building, I ran through two exercises in my head: firstly, how could I escape in a hurry if the need arose, and secondly, if I needed to destroy the structure, how would I do it?

"He didn't mention an external stopcock," Paige said. "But I guess I didn't ask."

"Have you got his number?"

"Uh... In my phone." I stared at her, and eventually she got the message. "It's, uh... Here it is. Niall. Niall-like-the-river Docherty."

She read out the number, and I typed it into my own phone. Dialled. It rang once, twice, ten bloody times... What was the point of having a mobile phone if you weren't going to answer it?

Finally, someone picked up. "Aye?"

"Niall Docherty?"

"That's right."

"I hear you're the man to call if there's a plumbing issue?"

"Aye, hen." Hen? I didn't have a fucking beak. "What's the problem?"

"A friend of mine is staying at Glendoon Hall. I understand—"

"That crazy wee lassie living out in the stable?"

"Yup, that's right. I understand you've already spoken with her about the stopcock—or rather, the lack of one—but if we can get the floor shored up, would you be willing to take another look?"

"Not for all the whisky in Islay. You're not from around these parts, are you?" Gee, had my accent given it away? "Here's my advice—go back to London, and take that poor bairn with you. The Beast of Glendoon roams around after dark, and that ramshackle shed isn't safe for folks like you."

"Folks like us? Do you mean foreigners? Or women?"

"No need to get testy." *Oh, I think there is.* "I'm just saying that fixing up a place like Glendoon Hall is a man's job, and no man in his right mind would take it on."

Really? Well, we'd see about that.

"Thanks for your time, Mr. Docherty."

Fuck.

6

EMMY

"Okay, so we need a new plumber." I turned to Sky. "And you can stop laughing."

She didn't. And how the hell was I meant to find a decent plumber? I'd have to call Bradley, but Bradley had gone to visit a friend in New York this weekend, which meant he'd be asleep right now and probably hung-over when he woke up.

Great.

When I opened the door to Paige's stable, three small brown things shot out. Mice? Baby rats? Mutant spiders? They bolted into a snaking mass of ivy and disappeared.

Just great.

Lying awake in the early hours, I'd had a vague idea that we could convert part of the stable block into something more habitable if the main house was a lost cause. Sewerage could be a problem, but many stable yards had water and mains electricity already installed, and some had grooms' accommodation too. Hell, back in Virginia, my horse had central heating and cable TV, courtesy of Bradley. And a house like this would've had grooms. Lord and Lady Whatever wouldn't have mucked out their own nags.

But no such luck. The only tap was dry, dangling wires were an invitation to electrocution, and the staff must've slept elsewhere.

"Maybe in the cottage up the hill?" Paige suggested when I mentioned it. "The croft, the lady in the grocery store called it, but I've never found out exactly where it is. Never really looked." She shuddered. "I'm not going up there alone."

"Who owns the land at the back?"

"Mostly me, I think? The contract said the house came with ninety-five acres, but I'm not sure where it ends or even how big that is."

"You literally just stay in the stable the whole time?"

"It's either that or sleep in my car. I tried that once, and a security guard at the university hammered on the windshield in the middle of the night and nearly gave me a heart attack."

"Where do you shower?"

"The changing room in the sports complex."

"We need to get the water connected here."

"I just don't have the money for that."

"It's not for you to worry about."

"But how—"

"Fletcher's brother is an amateur philanthropist. Your job today is to pack enough gear to stay in a hotel for a few weeks, and while you're doing that, me and Sky can make ourselves useful and take a look for the external stopcock. If we can find it, that'll be one less excuse for a plumber to come up with."

"I can't afford a hotel either."

"The cost is our concern, not yours."

"The library's open twenty-four hours, so I figured I might be able to sleep somewhere in the evenings and then go there at night."

"It won't come to that. Trust me, it won't come to that. Pack your gear while the two of us go for a walk around."

Seventeen years of training in the deadly arts, everything

from desert survival to sniping to improvising an explosive device with household objects, and now I was about to spend the morning searching for a bloody stopcock.

"You take me to all the best places," Sky said.

"As the US Navy would say, it's not just a job, it's an adventure. C'mon—if there is a stopcock, it'll be down by the road."

Honestly, I'd fought my way through jungles that were less overgrown. Narrow animal tracks wound through the grounds, but stray from one of those and you were straight into a tangle of gorse and dead bracken and brambles and all-encompassing ivy. And if the thorns didn't get you, there was a good chance of breaking an ankle in a rabbit hole. But as always, I'd come prepared, and I hacked at the undergrowth with my machete.

"It's probably under this layer of sludge." Sky poked at rotting leaf litter with the toe of her boot. "We'll never find it."

"We might need to come back with actual equipment."

"Won't the water company have a map or something?"

"Apparently not."

Paige had tried writing to them, and they denied all knowledge. Said that if the stopcock was on the property, it was the homeowner's responsibility. But at least they'd confirmed that Glendoon Hall was connected to the public supply. Unlike in England, unmetered water charges were bundled up into the council tax bill, so the previous owner of Glendoon Hall had kept the account current through the years.

A crumbling wall ran along the front boundary, six feet high with another foot of ivy draped over the top, the leaves festooned with cobwebs. A track ran parallel, and I ambled along it a little way, eyes on the dirt.

"There's too much undergrowth for ground-penetrating radar." How did I know that? Because Bradley's boyfriend was an archaeologist, and occasionally, I managed to stay awake through a conversation with him. "Too many tree roots."

"What about a metal detector?"

"A magnetometer would work as long as the pipes have iron in them."

"What else would they be made of? Not plastic in a place this old, surely?"

"Could be lead."

"Isn't that poisonous?"

"Life expectancies were lower in those days."

Sky kicked at a pile of leaves. "When I was sixteen, I lived in this old warehouse with a bunch of hippies, and one of them used this stick thing to find stuff. Dowsing, he called it."

"Stuff?"

"My phone, a dead rat that was stinking the place out, Gary's weed... Stuff."

"Fascinating. Why are you telling me this?"

"He said the stick could find water too."

"He was a hustler?"

"Yeah, on the streets, but not at home."

Bullshit. Maybe he didn't ask Sky for money, but he was still a hustler.

"So what are you suggesting? That we call your hippie friend and ask him to find the stopcock?"

Sky snorted. "Like I know where he is now. But he said anyone could do the stick thing, and..." She waved a hand at the surroundings. "There are plenty of trees, aren't there?"

Oh boy, this was gonna be good. I patted my pocket to make sure I had my phone. The folks back home could use a good laugh, and a picture painted a thousand words.

"Well, sure. Go right ahead. Want me to cut a stick for you, or would you rather do that yourself?"

"I thought *you* could try it," Sky said.

"Me? Why me?"

"Because you're the boss."

"And I'm delegating. If you believe in witchcraft, then you can demonstrate." I leaned against a tree, crossed my arms and ankles. "Please, be my guest."

"Yeah, so maybe we could revisit the metal detector idea?"

"No way. You're not getting out of this that easy."

Sky glared at me. "Fine. *Fine.*"

"Do you need to cast a spell on the stick first? Should I find a cauldron?"

She gave me an Agincourt salute as she stomped off into the trees, and I fired off a text to Hallie.

Me: Can you ask around at the office and see if anyone knows a good plumber? And by good, I mean tenacious. This place is a bloody nightmare.

Twigs cracked, and I stifled a laugh. Several years ago, we'd turned our attention to succession planning at Blackwood, and in all that time, Sky was the only person I'd considered might make a worthy protégé. Black—my husband—had his nephew, Rafael, ready to follow in his footsteps. In Slater, we'd found an excellent sniper for Carmen to train. We still needed to find an expert in executive protection to work alongside Nick and an electronics-slash-explosives genius to share Nate's basement lair, but we had time on our side.

And Sky still had a lot to learn.

She picked up the technical aspects of the job quickly, and she had the right instincts, but there was a hint of naivety lurking under the surface. On a scale of nought to Paige, I put her at a one, but we needed to get her closer to zero.

Ghosts and monsters and magic freaking sticks...

Yeah, right.

My phone pinged.

Hallie: Sure, I'll ask around.

Me: How's the DNA hunt going?

Hallie: We're waiting for Jake Burns to eat lunch, and we have a plan for Clare Muir.

Me: Dair behaving himself?

Hallie: Impeccably.

Good. Once, Dair had worn his reputation as a ladies' man with pride, but he'd dialled back on the charm since he had a kid. Not because he was off the market—the relationship had been over in weeks, by all accounts—but because he put his daughter's needs first. Plus he was a damn good investigator, and he had a kind heart. When Hallie had needed a temporary partner who'd take care of her, I'd figured Dair was the right man for the job.

"Hey!" Sky shouted. "Come and take a gander at this."

Ah, fuck. If a miracle had happened and Sky and her twig had managed to find the bloody stopcock, I was going to look like a right pillock. Humble pie was my least favourite meal. I'd eat it if I had to, but it gave me indigestion.

"Did you find water?" I followed her gaze to the ground at her feet, fighting the urge to roll my eyes at the Y-shaped stick in her hand. "What the fuck?"

They were footprints. Well, paw prints.

"Paige was right. The Beast of Glendoon exists."

"Oh, for crying out loud. Those are probably from a dog."

"They're the size of dinner plates."

Side plates, but okay, they were slightly on the large side.

"A Great Dane, then."

Sky folded her arms. "You just don't want to admit that I'm right and there's some kind of *thing* in these woods."

Because she was wrong. My lips curved into a grin, and I held out a hand. "Fifty quid says there's no *thing*."

She hesitated for a moment, and I thought she might back down, but no. She had guts, and she stood behind her convictions.

"You're on." Ah, then she realised. "Shit."

"Oh yeah, honey. You need proof."

Sky pointed at the footprint.

"Close, but no cigar."

"Then how?"

"I hope you brought your thermal underwear."

"Huh?" Realisation dawned. "Wait, you want to stay out here overnight?"

"Yup."

"But... But... Can't we just set out cameras or something? Motion detectors?"

"Where's the fun in that?"

"You're insane."

"Tell me something I don't know." I snapped a dozen pictures of the paw prints, then slung an arm over her shoulders. "C'mon, we can sing campfire songs and make s'mores."

"What about sleep?"

"Plenty of time for that when we're dead."

After the fact, I'd look back and wish we could have traded Sky's dowsing stick for a crystal ball. Or left Fletcher to do his own damn dirty work. But without the benefit of hindsight, I waved a hand towards the stable block, oblivious.

Who needed a vacation anyway?

"Let the adventure begin."

7

HALLIE

Jake Burns worked behind the counter of a builders' merchant in the town of Bonnyrigg, a half hour south of Edinburgh. Dair had meandered into the store earlier to check that Jake was indeed there, and now we were the proud owners of a hammer, a spirit level, and three kinds of nails. Maybe Paige could make use of them? Although if Emmy's text was anything to go by, we should have bought bathroom sealant and a spare faucet.

"Coming up to lunchtime," Dair said.

I already knew that. My stomach had been grumbling for the past hour. Skipping breakfast in favour of an extra twenty minutes' sleep had seemed like a good idea at the time, but now I was starving, and unlike Ford, Dair didn't keep a package of candy in his glove compartment.

"Hallelujah." The big question was whether Jake brown-bagged it or bought lunch from a local eatery. There were two nearby—a greasy spoon and a chain café. "I'd trade my soul for a sandwich."

"Well, Burns has already seen my face today, so you might just get your wish."

"You mean I'll be following him?"

"Look on the bright side—you get to buy food instead of carpentry supplies."

"What we need is plumbing supplies."

Dair raised an eyebrow.

"For Glendoon Hall. I don't suppose you know a good plumber?"

"Oh, aye, my cousin Ross is a plumber."

If I'd learned one thing about Dair this morning, it was that he had a seemingly inexhaustible supply of relatives. Brothers, sisters, nieces, nephews, aunts, uncles, cousins...

"How many cousins do you have?"

"At last count? Seventeen, but there's another on the way."

Growing up, it had just been me and my mom. I'd never fought with a sibling or dropped by a grandma's home for apple pie or celebrated the arrival of a new cousin. The idea of a caring family had been as mythical as the Beast of Glendoon itself. But Dair seemed tight with his clan. When we'd discussed the Muir cluster this morning, he'd quickly roped in his cousin Maeve to help. Something along the lines of, "Aye, would you look at this? Maeve and Clare go to the same school. Clare's a couple of years older, but Maeve's a sneaky wee thing."

"Will Maeve keep quiet about the case?" I'd asked.

If it became the subject of schoolyard gossip, that could be a problem.

"Och, she's got designs on becoming an investigator herself. Following in my footsteps, so to speak. Aye, she'll keep her mouth shut."

So we had a kid doing our dirty work, and all for the price of a six-pack of IRN-BRU and a package of Tunnock's Teacakes. I still wasn't sure what a teacake was, but Dair informed me it was neither tea nor cake and there were plenty in the kitchen back at the office.

Anyhow, getting back to the plumber situation...

"Is Ross..." What was the word Emmy used? "Uh, tenacious?"

"He was a Royal Marine. Tenacity runs through his blood."

"He went from the Marines to plumbing?"

"Don't knock plumbing. There's good money in it, and Ross always was good with his hands."

"Do you think he'd be willing to take a look at the water supply at Glendoon Hall?"

"As long as it's daylight, I reckon he'd give it the once-over."

Well, solving that problem had been unexpectedly easy. "Can I get his number for Emmy?"

Dair chuckled. "I'd better call and warn him first. Ah, here's your man."

Jake Burns ambled around the side of the building, attention firmly fixed on the phone in his hand as he set off along the street. Records showed he was thirty-seven, but if I'd had to guess, I'd have put him a little older. Life had worn him down. Life plus two ex-wives and four kids. We'd put together a brief bio, and the most interesting part was that one of those wives had been American. Jake had spent several years living in Chattanooga, Tennessee, which wasn't a million miles from Richmond, Virginia. We hadn't managed to pin down the dates precisely, but it was possible some of that time had overlapped with Mila Carmody's disappearance. When Valerie had given me the list of clusters we needed to check, plus her initial research, chills had run up my spine when I read her notes on Jake.

Could I be watching a murderer?

I kept my distance as we walked out of the retail park,

heading toward food. Jake didn't look behind him, not once. He barely even looked in front of him. Whatever was on his phone was far more interesting, and he nearly tripped over another guy's dog. Words were exchanged. I couldn't hear them, but the dog guy's hand gesture left me in no doubt that Jake was a wanker. If nothing else, working with Emmy had broadened my repertoire of insults, especially the British ones.

My heart sank as we headed past the nice café, then lifted again as Jake pushed open the door to the greasy spoon. A plate of fries would be better than no food at all.

Uh-oh. So much for keeping a low profile... The place was packed, and every single head turned to stare at me, probably because I was the only female in the joint apart from the two ladies behind the counter. Even they did a double take. Gee, this was awkward, but I joined the back of the line behind Jake. What other choice did I have?

He ordered a cheese-and-tomato toastie to go, then looked me up and down, more nosy than pervy. "Yer not from around here?"

"Uh, no, I'm a student in Edinburgh."

"At the university?"

"That's right."

"What ye doing in Bonnyrigg? Lost, are ye?"

"Oh, I'm just exploring the local area."

"Ye'd be better off headin' north. Goin' to visit Nessie." Jake cackled at his own non-joke.

"I already went to Glendoon. That filled my quota of mythical monsters for this week."

"Oh, aye, the Beast of Glendoon, but there's nowt mythical about it. Ye don't want to go there at night."

"Really? You think the rumours are true?"

"The Beast exists, sure enough. My sister's boyfriend's pal saw it right across the wynd from the Glendoon Inn. Two glowing eyes watching him from the trees."

So he'd been drinking? Figured.

"Just the eyes? He didn't see the rest of it?"

"Och, no. He ran off down the hill and fell in the burn."

"The burn? What was on fire? Did he get injured?"

Jake fixed his gaze on me for a long second, then sucked in a breath and began to guffaw. What? What was so funny?

"I don't get it?"

"Angus," he said, smacking the guy in front of him on the shoulder. "Angus, this 'ere Yankee thinks the burn's ablaze. Call the fire brigade!"

Why were they laughing at me? And I wasn't a freaking Yankee either.

"Actually, I was born in southern Kentucky."

Jake went into a coughing fit, and Angus thumped him on the back. A big glob of spittle flew out of Jake's mouth and landed on my lapel, which was revolting, but now I could smile too. One DNA sample: collected.

"Would one of you mind enlightening me?"

"A burn's a brook," Angus choked out. "It's *water*."

Ah. Right. Why couldn't these people just speak English? "Okay, I understand now. Thanks."

"Yer welcome, lassie."

Thankfully, the lady behind the counter saved me from further ridicule.

"Jake, your toastie's done. Angus, I'll bring your baked potato over in a minute." Then she focused on me. "Ignore those two, my love. What can I get you?"

"Two portions of fries to go, please."

"Salt and sauce?"

"Uh, I guess?"

Soon, I was on my way back to Dair's car with two styrofoam containers of chunky fries covered in runny brown liquid. I'd lost my appetite now, but Dair practically snatched his portion out of my hands.

"You're a lifesaver. Did you get the sample?"

"Yup."

"From a cup? A glass? A ketchup sachet?"

Everyone else had laughed at me already, so why not Dair? Thankfully, he didn't hork all over the windshield, and he also helped me to wriggle carefully out of my jacket and seal it into an evidence bag. One down, three to go. And when I risked trying one of the fries, they weren't actually too bad.

"What's in the sauce?" I asked.

"Nobody knows."

"Really?"

"Most chippies have their own secret recipe."

"So it could contain *anything*?"

"Probably won't kill you."

"*Probably*?"

"If you're not gonnae eat yours, pass them over."

Hmm... "Maybe I'll just have a couple."

Two hours later, I was still stuffed full of carbs. But I'd run into a mall to pick up a new jacket, and we were back at the office packaging the latest sample for the courier.

"Here you go," Dair said. "Coffee, a Tunnock's Teacake, and some good old-fashioned Scottish tablet."

"I don't think I can eat another thing."

And what was Scottish tablet? While Dair checked his messages, I took a second to google and found it was basically sugar.

"We can pack you a wee doggy bag to take away with you," he said, coming back to the conversation. "And Ross says he can skip the footie tomorrow and go to Glendoon in the afternoon."

"He doesn't mind?"

"Kilmarnock's bound to lose anyway. Check with Emmy what time she'll be there?"

I typed out a text and got a reply back a minute later.

Emmy: He can come whenever—me and Sky are gonna be here all night.

Me: What? Why?

Had they both lost their minds?

Emmy: We made a small wager. Got enough clothing? We're at the outdoor store if you need anything.

Me: I just bought a new jacket.

Emmy: What happened to the old one?

Me: A potential suspect spit a DNA sample onto it.

Emmy: Nice work. What about the second sample?

Me: Apparently a kid named Maeve is handling it on Monday. Dair swears it'll work out, but I'm ready to step in if necessary.

Emmy: Maeve? You might as well put your feet up.

Me: You know her?

Emmy: Yeah, she's basically the office mascot. Are you coming to Glendoon tonight?

I wanted to say no. I really did. But I was a Blackwood girl, and Blackwood girls didn't cower in the face of legendary fiends. Besides, I'd bet my last package of M&Ms that Emmy would be armed up the wazoo.

Me: Can you pick me up from the office?

Emmy: Be there in 30 mins :)

8

EMMY

lendoon had precisely one option when it came to accommodation. According to the sign outside, parts of the Glendoon Inn dated back to the sixteenth century, and I suspected the decor did too. Downstairs was a pub, and there were half a dozen bedrooms above for visitors and patrons too drunk to make it home safely.

Although Sky, Hallie, and I wouldn't be sleeping there overnight, we booked a room so we could get a hot shower and breakfast in the morning. Sure, we could've barbecued a rabbit or two, but since this was meant to be a sort-of-vacation, I figured we deserved a proper fry-up if we were still alive. And no, I didn't think the Beast of Glendoon was going to pick us off. It was a myth. But the temperature was forecast to plummet, and the risk of hypothermia was very real.

We planned to camp out in Paige's stable, taking it in turns to rest while another kept watch. Thanks to the outdoor store, we had decent sleeping bags and appropriate clothing, plus I'd swung by the office and grabbed a few extra supplies, roughly half of which were legal. Just because I didn't believe in a

53

folkloric creature with razor-sharp claws and burning embers for eyes—which was the absolute gospel truth according to Aileen, who ran the Glendoon Inn—didn't mean I'd forget my "be prepared" mantra. And Sky had nipped into an electronics store to buy a fancy digital camera because she was determined to catch the Beast in action. Mack—one of my besties and Blackwood's Head of Cyber—was under strict instructions to report any requests for Photoshop work directly to me.

"Ready?" I asked Sky and Hallie.

Sky took one last wistful look around my room at the inn and sighed. Incidentally, Aileen also thought we were crackers for "sleeping rough in a bear pit" and she'd asked us to pay for the room in advance in case we didn't make it back. None of the locals went near the old place, apparently.

"Yeah, I'm ready," Sky said. "Who needs heating, anyway?"

"I bought a tabletop s'mores kit. Stop complaining."

"Can't we light a campfire?" Hallie asked.

"No go," Sky told her. "Wild animals won't come close if they see flames."

"So...isn't that a great reason to light a campfire?"

Nice try... "Ah, but Sky wants to catch the Beast."

And besides, we did have heating. Kind of. I'd given Paige's generator a good kick, and it had coughed and spluttered reluctantly into life. Theoretically, we wouldn't freeze to death inside unless it decided to quit again.

But in practice, the old stable had so many gaps in the walls that the fan heater barely took the edge off the chill. Was Paige cold-blooded? If I were in her shoes, I'd probably have gone into hibernation.

Hallie sank onto a newly purchased cot. "Why am I even here? I could have stayed in Edinburgh with Paige."

I knew why, and that was the reason she was working at Blackwood. Why Black had hand-picked her to join us, why we'd elevated her past colleagues who'd joined the company much earlier, and why Dan had taken Hallie under her wing to train personally. Hallie had the mix of courage, brains, and determination that we needed, plus an inbuilt curiosity that led her to ask the right questions. She didn't quit. Knock her down, and she'd always get up again. Sure, she sometimes needed a hand back onto her feet, but that's what the rest of us were there for.

"You're here because you want to be. Let's eat dinner, and then we can take shifts. Ninety minutes each, so nobody's out in the cold for too long. Who wants to go first?"

Hallie raised her hand. "I'd prefer to get it over with."

"And I'll go second," Sky said. "How does this s'mores thing work?"

"I think—" Hallie's phone rang with John Legend's "All of Me," and she blushed, so I figured it was Ford calling. "Uh, I should answer this."

She backed towards the far corner, cheeks turning bright red as Sky yelled, "Hi, Ford!"

I added my voice for good measure. The two lovebirds were well matched. I wasn't keen on cops in general, but I had to admit that Ford wasn't a total arsehole, and the new Richmond PD captain—Broussard—wasn't too awful either. Maybe in the future, we'd be able to coexist in peace rather than antagonising each other? Rubbing his predecessor up the wrong way had become almost a sport to me. Too bad he'd eaten a bullet. Nothing to do with me, I hasten to add, although if I'd known at the time just how young he liked his girlfriends, I'd gladly have helped him on his way.

The s'mores kit had a little gel burner included, and I set it on Paige's rickety table, hoping the laminate wouldn't scorch.

Although it wouldn't much matter if it did end up with a few marks. Whatever happened with our beast-hunting, she'd never live in this place in its current form again. Five minutes later, when Hallie had finished whispering sweet nothings to her new beau, we were roasting marshmallows on little bamboo skewers.

"I heard you're definitely moving in with Ford?" Sky said, arranging crackers on a paper plate.

"How do you know that?"

Yeah, how *did* she know that?

"Mercy told Rafael, and Rafael told me."

Good news travelled fast, as did Hallie and Ford's relationship. But their moving in together wasn't entirely unexpected—I'd been there when Mercy made the suggestion —and when you knew, you knew. Unless, of course, you were me or Sky. I'd dithered around for years before I finally got it on with Black, and Sky was currently doing the same with Rafael. Not that she realised it yet. No, she was happily shacked up with Asher, who was a nice guy, a really nice guy, just not *her* guy. I only hoped the eventual—and, in my opinion, inevitable—break-up wouldn't be too painful.

I might not have believed in cryptids, but where love was involved, I'd come to believe in fate.

"So, when's the wedding?" I asked, and Hallie turned the colour of a beetroot.

"Who told you about that?"

What the actual fuck? "I was joking. You *are* getting married?"

"No! I mean, not yet."

"Not yet?"

"Well, I guess it was mentioned in passing."

"Honey, marriage isn't the sort of thing a guy mentions in passing. It's a big deal."

Sky stared nonchalantly at the ceiling. "Says the woman who got married drunk in Vegas."

"Yeah, well, I needed a green card. Hallie's situation is totally different." My marshmallow was nicely singed, and I sandwiched it between crackers with a lump of chocolate. "Spill. I have a good bottle of Scotch here if that would help."

Now Sky focused on my face. "You brought alcohol to a stake-out? Why do I get the feeling you're not taking this seriously?"

"Sky, my sweet, we're on a stake-out for a *mutant zoo animal*. Alcohol is practically mandatory."

Hallie held out a plastic tumbler. "Make mine a double."

I fished the bottle out of my newly acquired backpack and poured everyone a generous measure.

"Plus we're supporting the local economy. This here is Glendoon Single Malt, distilled at the other end of the village. Cheers."

And it was surprisingly good. Black was something of a whisky connoisseur, and although I preferred gin, I could still pick out a decent Scotch. This was a good colour, full-bodied with a hint of smoke. Before we left, I'd have to buy a case to take back to Virginia.

"So, where were we?" I asked.

Sky might have complained about the Scotch, but she'd still drunk it, and now she grinned.

"Hallie was spilling the details of her maybe-engagement."

"Guys, we're *not* engaged. I was just a bit nervous about... you know..."—she lowered her voice to a whisper—"going to bed with him, and he said we could wait as long as I wanted, and he'd put a ring on my finger first if it made me feel more comfortable."

Yup, Ford was definitely her Mr. Right. "And you didn't jump all over that?"

"It, uh, wasn't necessary. I got distracted, so I only held out for, like, five more minutes."

Sky raised an eyebrow. "Distracted by what?"

What do you know? There was a shade above beetroot. "I shouldn't say."

"No, you should. I'm *great* at keeping secrets. Right, Emmy?"

"Right."

That part was definitely true. Sky was one of only three people who knew just how close I'd come to removing Black's balls with a potato peeler earlier in the year, and she hadn't breathed a word.

"It's no big deal. Ford has a piercing, that's all, and it caught me by surprise."

"A piercing? Where?" Sky asked.

"I promised I wouldn't say."

Oh, for fuck's sake. "It's in his cock."

Hallie's mouth dropped open. "How do you—"

"Because if it was anywhere else, then firstly, we would've seen it, and secondly, you would've told us." I shuddered a little. "Anyhow, rather you than me."

"You don't like piercings?"

"Down there? I'm not a fan. Don't you find it uncomfortable?"

She got this dreamy look in her eyes. "It's magic. But wait... Who did you...? Not Black...?"

"Oh, fuck no. Nick."

Sky and Hallie both choked on s'mores. I whacked them on the back, perhaps slightly harder than was necessary.

"Nick?" Sky asked. "*Nick* has his dick pierced?"

"I thought that was pretty much common knowledge, but I guess not. We made a bet, and he lost, otherwise I'd be the one sitting here with pierced privates."

A foolish wager, incidentally, was also the reason President

James Harrison had a tattoo of an eagle on his ass. He hadn't learned from Nick's mistake, and if you looked really close—and *maybe* I'd had that pleasure—you'd see the eagle had my nickname hidden on one foot.

"I need to sign up for the office gossip network," Sky said. "Who do I see about that?"

"No one. What you actually need to do is finish eating so you can get some sleep before your watch."

"So who else has baubles on their bits?"

"How the hell should I know? Eat!"

Decades of abandonment had led Glendoon Hall to become a haven for wildlife. During my silent vigil, deer tiptoed in the murky gloom beyond the stable block, a badger meandered around the cobbled yard, and two hedgehogs shuffled through the icy slush not five metres from my feet. Owls swooped low overhead. My breath steamed. When we'd dropped by the office earlier, I'd also raided the collection of scuba gear and picked out a diver's thermal undersuit, so I was basically wearing a sleeping bag, but I still couldn't feel my feet.

One shift down, one to go...

At least I'd get to see the sunrise, and I bet it would be beautiful. For all Glendoon's faults, I had to concede it was situated in a stunning part of the world, scenery-wise. I shifted in the folding chair to get comfortable, then wrapped a dark-grey scarf across my face. Blended into the background. Settled in for the wait.

The rest of the night was uneventful. At the changeover, Sky seemed somewhat sullen at the prospect of losing her fifty quid, and I was fairly sure Hallie regretted passing up the five-star digs in favour of frostbite and boredom. But in the early hours, soon after I'd started my second shift, I felt the tiniest prickle at the base of my spine. A barely-there niggle that said "look out."

Over the years, I'd learned to trust my instincts. They'd saved me more times than I could count. And although nothing moved, and the only sounds were the wind and an occasional bird call, I knew there was *something* out there.

Something that wasn't an owl or a deer or a badger or a hedgehog.

Slowly, slowly, I turned on the thermal imaging scope in my lap, but before it had a chance to warm up, a light on the hill caught my eye. No, not *a* light. Two glowing red orbs that watched me without moving for a few seconds, then vanished in the blink of an eye.

Ah, fuck.

I picked up a pair of night-vision goggles and jammed them on, and sure enough, there was movement in the trees. Branches swishing against a still background, the movement too jerky for the wind to be the cause, a shadow flitting quietly through the forest. What was it? Man or beast? I couldn't tell from this distance, but the pattern wasn't expansive enough for a ten-foot-tall behemoth.

Softly, softly, I slipped back into the stable.

"Sky, take my place."

She was awake in an instant. "What is it?"

"Something's on the hill. Stay on guard while I head over for a closer look."

"Is that a good idea?"

"Probably not. Wake Hallie and be ready to back me up."

"If you're chasing after the Beast of Glendoon, then I should come with you."

"No, you should stay here unless I call you forward."

Sky knew how to move in an urban environment, but in this terrain? She lacked experience. Soon, she'd head off to

South America with Rafael to learn the joys of jungle warfare, and after that, we'd get her into the forest, the desert, the steppes, the tundra.

What about me? Well, I'd had half a lifetime of practice, and a couple of months ago, I'd worked with an old buddy of Black's on a rescue mission. That guy moved like a ghost. A ghoul. A military magician. So I'd wheedled and cajoled and he'd let me tag along on a training exercise with his girls, and by "girls," I meant the Choir. Pale, aka Church, headed up a clandestine programme to create, well… The Choir was basically a team of women with the skills and guts to do the impossible. Black said the government wanted clones of yours truly, and I guess I should have been flattered, but there was always room for me to learn. And it had been a fun trip, four of us sleeping under the stars and shooting at a team of fake terrorists. The final score had been Church, Valkyrie, Dusk, and Dice seventeen, tangos nil.

Hmm. Maybe I should chat Pale up and see if he'd take Sky for a week or two… It was a thought.

The forest wasn't so dense up on the hill—not as many brambles, probably because a thick carpet of needles from the evergreens killed off everything else that tried to grow there. I slipped between the trees like a phantom with the thermal scope held to my eye and a weapon within easy reach. Today, I had the choice of a taser or a semi-automatic pistol, both most definitely illegal for a civilian in Scotland, but I figured I'd rather break the law than come to a nasty end beneath the firs.

A flash of white showed up on the scope, and I stilled. Thermal imaging was great at telling you that there was a creature ahead, but not so good at identifying what that creature might be. I flipped down the night-vision goggles as a deer stepped out of the bushes. False alarm. If I was going to make a habit of this, I'd have to get better equipment sent up from London—a set of integrated thermal/NV goggles, for starters. Sure, they were military kit, but guess who owned shares in the manufacturer? Free samples, baby.

The deer carried on its merry way, no haste, no heed, and disappeared into the bushes. In the moment's pause, I realised my sixth sense had stopped ringing the alarm bells too. That niggle in my spine, it had eased off. Whatever had been out in the forest, it wasn't here anymore.

And now… Now, it was time for breakfast.

9

EMMY

"That's a nice bit of kit." Ross pointed at my shiny new goggles. "Better than anything we used to get."

Ah, yes. It turned out our plumber was former military. Well, he was still in the reserves, but now he spent most of his time fighting water leaks instead of the enemy. And right now, he was in Paige's stable at Glendoon, studying the contents of the load-out bags two interns had driven up from London. The interns themselves were now ensconced in my and Sky's former Edinburgh hotel rooms with a generous meal allowance, a promise of time off in lieu, and an instruction not to get too drunk tonight. And I was preparing for another stake-out.

Yes, I'd told Sky about the glowing red "eyes," and no, she hadn't shut up about them all day. But this afternoon, we still had one last blessed hour of daylight left to walk Ross around the property and see what he might be able to do to help make it habitable, and that took priority over stalking a mythical beast.

"Just one benefit of the private sector," I told him. "You never considered going into the security industry?"

He shook his head. "Decided I wanted to be my own boss."

"You don't mind working alone?"

"I'm not really alone. Four of us left the Marines at the same time, and we have... I guess you could call it an alliance. Marc's an electrician, AJ's a carpenter, and Griff does brickwork and plastering. We work together when we need to. Our specialty is refurbing properties for buy-to-let landlords."

Hmm. "So you know a good electrician?"

"I do."

"What's he doing this week?"

"Drowning his sorrows, probably."

"For any particular reason?"

It was Dair who rolled his eyes. He'd shown up too, presumably out of nosiness.

"The usual," he said. "Woman trouble. Marc's got an on-again, off-again girlfriend."

"And they're currently off?"

"Naw, on. Every time they split up, she sends him on a guilt trip over something or another and he agrees to give it another go."

"Plus this week's job got cancelled," Ross added. "A developer hired us to fix up a row of cottages near Cowdenbeath, but my brother-in-law's uncle's boss heard on the grapevine that the fella's about to go bankrupt, so we asked him to pay for the materials upfront. Funnily enough, he declined to do that." Ross shrugged. "Lucky escape."

One man's loss was another woman's gain. "If Marc can provide some input on the state of the electrics in this place, I'll pay the going rate for his time. What did Dair tell you about the situation here?"

"Just that a young lady bought the place by accident, and it's not particularly habitable." Ross turned to Sky. "Was that you, lass?"

Sky managed to look both horrified and insulted at the same time. "Hell no."

His gaze landed on Hallie next, and she held up both hands. "Not me either."

"Paige has been trying to deal with this on her own for months," I explained. "She's run down, and she's exhausted, so we sent her to a hotel." Hallie had called her several times today, and the interns checked on her earlier as well. All she wanted to do right now was sleep, and who could criticise her for that? "But thinking long term, we need to find her somewhere habitable to stay, and I was wondering if we could do something with the stable block?"

"Turn it into a home, you mean?"

"Exactly."

"Aye, but you'd need planning permission for change of use. Daresay you'd get it because anything's better than this eyesore, but it wouldn't be the work of five minutes. Then you'd have to sort out the sewerage." Ross waved towards the cobbled yard. "That lot would need digging up."

"Any other suggestions as to how we could approach this?"

"You'd be better off renovating a section of the big house." *Hoose.* He pronounced it like "goose." "At least then you wouldn't need to worry about permissions, just building regs, and unless tree roots have damaged the pipes, you should have sewerage from there too. Does this place have a septic tank? A cesspool? Its own sewage treatment plant? Can't imagine it's connected to mains drainage out here."

Did he honestly expect me to answer that question?

"You're asking the wrong person. How long would renovations take? It's a bloody mess inside by all accounts, and Paige is only here until next June."

Ross sucked on his teeth. "A wee while, I'd say. Hows about"—hoos aboot—"parking a mobile home out the back here. Then all we'd need to do is reinstate the utilities and hook everything up. What's your budget?"

"The budget's under discussion, but a mobile home plus your labour to help with the installation would be doable."

We'd still have the problem of the accidental purchase to deal with, but surely an estate agent could manage to offload the place in the next eight months? Hell, Nick would probably cover the losses if Fletcher asked him to.

"Can we take a look around the house? See what we're dealing with?" Ross tipped his chin at the tap in the corner of the stable yard. "That doesn't work?"

"Nothing works, and sure, we can take a look in the house. But I understand there's a hole in the floor that the previous plumber nearly fell in, so tread carefully."

To give Ross his credit, he didn't run screaming. No, he found a torch in his van and stood by my side when I unlocked the back door. Paige had given me the key, but it was the first time I'd ventured inside.

We found ourselves in a small vestibule. The sun was already kissing the horizon, leaving the rooms of Glendoon Hall blanketed in shadows and cobwebs. The smell of damp permeated throughout, along with the musty stink of rat urine and an underlying aroma of dead mouse. In the near-silence, I heard the pitter-patter of tiny paws running overhead. To our right, stairs led up to the first floor, flanked by what had once been ornate wooden banisters, and straight ahead was the aforementioned hole. I shined a light inside, and the beam went deeper than I thought it would.

"There's a basement."

"That's not a basement, it's a dungeon," Sky said from behind.

Through an open door straight ahead, I spotted an old Belfast sink—that was the kitchen. I nodded towards it.

"Stopcock?" I suggested.

Ross nodded back. "There's a good chance of that."

"Under the sink?"

"Aye."

Would the edges of the floor hold my weight? I inched forward, keeping my back against the wall where possible, and although there were a few ominous creaks, nothing gave way. I used the same trick to skirt around the kitchen until I reached the sink, then crouched to check in the cupboard beneath it. The door came off in my hand, and a platoon of spiders scuttled out, fat little fuckers with hairy legs. Good thing Bradley wasn't here, or we'd have been plucking him out of the basement by now.

I peered into their lair and cursed. "There's no stopcock here."

"Might be in another cupboard," Ross called back. "Or under the stairs, or in a bathroom, or a utility room, or down in that cellar."

Fan-bloody-tastic.

Gingerly, I searched the other cupboards and found three desiccated rats, a bunch of mouse corpses, several old mixing bowls, and the rusting remains of a bread bin. Still no stopcock. I'd spotted the basement stairs as I crossed to the kitchen, but half of them were missing. We'd need to find a ladder if we planned to go down there.

I reversed course and headed back the way I'd come. There were more rooms off to the left, storerooms perhaps, but when I played the torch beam over the floor in that direction, it looked in worse shape than the rest. I suspected rain had been coming in the rear windows for years before Paige boarded them up, and the constant damp of the Scottish winters hadn't been kind to the timbers.

Back in the vestibule, I decided to head deeper into the building. Not because I had any particular confidence that I'd find the stopcock—it was like hunting for a black cat in a coal cellar—but because I was curious.

Once, this had been a grand old building, and an air of melancholy surrounded me when I tiptoed into the reception hall. The moulded—and mouldy—ceiling was a full two floors above me, although chunks of plaster littered the tiles at my feet. Hmm, the tiles... This floor wasn't made from wood. The basement didn't extend to the entire footprint of the building.

"Guys, there's a stone floor in here. If we can open up the front door or a window on the other side of the house, you should be able to climb through onto solid ground."

Although Sky couldn't wait that long. She appeared at my elbow, gazing at the massive columns that supported the ceiling.

"Fancy."

"Yeah, it was once."

A split staircase led down from the first floor, and above it, a rainbow of light filtered in through a waterfall of ivy. The windows were stained glass, although I couldn't see the pattern in the darkness.

We ventured farther and found a music room. A grand piano sat broken in one corner, one leg collapsed but two more hanging on. Tattered curtains stirred in the breeze, and something stirred in my chest. Glendoon Hall had been beautiful once.

"Who would leave a neat old castle like this to decay?" Sky asked.

"No idea, but it's a shame."

A crying shame.

Once we'd lost the daylight, we retreated outside and made a plan. Ross and his friends would come back tomorrow with tools, a ladder, and appropriate safety gear, and we'd explore Glendoon Hall properly.

But this evening, I withdrew to the Glendoon Inn for dinner with Sky and Hallie before we resumed our stake-out. Sky was still determined to win our bet, and I had to admit that I was curious about what I'd seen last night. And also about the history of Glendoon Hall.

When Aileen set a steaming dish of mac and cheese in front of me, I motioned for her to stay.

"Have you got a minute?"

She glanced around the pub, but it was quiet tonight. Half a dozen men stood in a group at the bar, and two tables of people were eating, but nobody was waiting for service. In fact, several of the men looked as if they'd struggle to lift a glass. Two of them would be on the floor if the bar wasn't holding them up, and the red-headed loudmouth the others referred to as "Boss" was slurring so badly that I could hardly understand a word he said. Something about whisky and a chainsaw? Always a winning combination.

"Aye, I've got a minute," Aileen said. "You want me to sit?"

"Please. Can you tell us what happened at Glendoon Hall? How did it fall into ruin?"

"A real tragedy, that was. All happened before I was born, but my grandpa told me the story. It's said that Donal Wallace —the seventeenth Laird of Glendoon—was a descendant of William Wallace, and—"

"William Wallace?" Sky asked. "The dude out of *Braveheart*?"

"That's him, although they took a few liberties with that film, let me tell you."

"Wait, it was based on a true story? I thought Hollywood made it up."

"Parts of it were true, and Donal Wallace had courage just as William did. When war broke out, Donal was the first to volunteer to fight for his country, but like so many men, he didn't make it back home."

"Which war are we talking about?" I asked.

"World War II. As I said, before my time. Some say his spirit lives on in the Beast of Glendoon."

Please, don't give Sky any more ideas. "So he died, and his home went to wrack and ruin? Didn't he have an heir?"

"Two sons, but they were just wee bairns at the time, and when their mother died of a broken heart, they were sent to live with relatives. Neither of them wanted to come back, seeing as the Lady's ghost still roams the hallways at night, but they couldn't bring themselves to sell the place either. So there it sat."

"Who did sell it?"

"The nineteenth laird." Aileen practically spat the words. "Rarely did he visit the village, and when he bothered to show up, he swanned around with that loud-mouthed wife of his as if he owned the whole place. Moira at the general store heard he needed the cash to pay off his gambling debts. Plus his wife has expensive tastes. Designer this, designer that. We were hoping a new owner might restore the place, breathe some life back into Glendoon, but then that wee lassie bought the estate, and it seems she doesn't have the finances either."

"She's looking to sell, so you might get your wish."

"As long as it isn't one of those big developers who buys it just to knock it down."

"I'm not sure they'd be allowed to do that. What about planning permission?"

"Och, if a man has enough money, he can buy himself permission to do whatever he pleases." Okay, I had to give her that one, although I'd never demolish a nice old castle. "I've got old pictures of the place somewhere, from back in its heyday. Would you like to see them?"

"Yeah, if you don't mind. And can I get a dozen bottles of Glendoon Single Malt to take home with me? The twelve-year-old stuff I was drinking yesterday."

Aileen's eyes lit up. "I'll see what I can do. If I don't have a dozen here, I can pick up more from the distillery tomorrow."

"I'd appreciate it. Do you know if they ship overseas?"

"You'd have to ask Fergus. I expect they do, but for how much longer, I can't say."

"Why would they stop?"

"The distillery can't go on forever. Fergus wants to retire, and the equipment's on its last legs too."

"Equipment can be replaced. Expertise can be passed down to the next generation."

"What 'next generation'? Fergus's sons both moved away, one to Glasgow and the other to Edinburgh. Kids don't stick around in Glendoon. There's no jobs, no future, no hope. Money doesn't grow on trees, lass."

That wasn't entirely true. I part-owned a sweet little olive grove in Italy, and the oil went for a premium. Plus I had a citrus farm in Florida, and I'd invested in a banana plantation in Sri Lanka, although granted, that hadn't been done with profit in mind.

But I understood Aileen's sentiment.

And I also thought it would be a crying shame if the Glendoon Distillery closed its doors.

Food for thought.

But my dinner was getting cold, and I needed to fuel up for tonight.

We had a "monster" to catch.

71

10

EMMY

"What the hell was that?" Sky hissed.

Dair had called last night to say his daughter wanted to stay at his sister's place because his niece had just got a new Teen Dream doll, whatever one of those was, and his sister would take them both to school tomorrow. So did we want a hand?

I wasn't one to say no to the offer of additional labour, plus I figured he could drive Hallie back to Edinburgh in the morning, so he'd shown up with a sleeping bag and I'd changed around the shifts. Hallie and Dair had taken the first of the two-hour watches, and now it was me and Sky who were freezing our arses off in the stable yard, waiting for...

Well, it turned out to be a howl.

A decidedly canine howl, and not too dissimilar from the ones I'd listened to on YouTube earlier. Yes, okay, I'd been researching wolves. Not because I thought there was some mutant beast on the loose, but because I couldn't rule out the possibility that a regular wolf might have somehow been roaming the wilds of Scotland undetected for years. Officially, the last of the original Scottish wolves had been slain in 1680, but there were stories of more recent sightings. Plus there was a "re-wilding" project taking place farther up in the Highlands, and occasionally exotic pets escaped or got dumped when they grew too big.

"Might've been an animal."

I'd left my thermal goggles turned on and ready, sacrificing battery life for instant imaging capability, and I scanned the hillside along with Sky.

"Not just any animal. There's something up there." She pointed at a white blob to our right. A heat source. "See?"

I did see. From the size, it could have been a deer or a dog or, okay, a wolf. But I couldn't make out any wings, so I had to take that as a good sign.

"Want to take a closer look?"

She had to learn sometime, right? And this afternoon while we waited for Ross to arrive, I'd taken her for a walk in the trees and given her a few pointers on moving quietly. Not that we'd need to stay quiet if we did spot a wolf. That was an invitation to attack. No, we'd make eye contact, act intimidating, and create as much noise as possible. I'd purchased a bulk pack of air horns, just in case.

If only it had been a giant cat we were hunting instead of a dog—I could have simply taken a laser pointer and an empty cardboard box for hours of fun.

"Uh, you mean go up there?" Sky asked.

"Don't chicken out now. It was you who wanted to play monster hunter."

I moved off quietly, taking the same route I'd walked yesterday. Sky stuck close behind, and I had to give her credit for not sounding like a herd of wildebeests. She hesitated as another howl sounded—I didn't see her do it, but I felt it. My sixth sense was working overtime in this environment.

But you know what I didn't feel? That same creepy-crawly spine tingle I'd experienced yesterday.

And when we finally caught up with the white blob, it was a bloody great deer. The instant it saw us, it stopped dead for a moment much as Sky had, then skedaddled into the undergrowth.

"False alarm," I whispered.

"Thank fuck."

"I'd expected you to sound slightly more disappointed."

"Right." Sky clutched a hand to her chest theatrically. "I'm heartbroken we didn't get eaten."

"No drama?" I asked Hallie and Dair at the next changeover.

When we'd told them about the howling, Hallie hadn't been thrilled at the thought of going outside, but she'd still taken her place beside Dair. They were both under orders to wake Sky and me if anything worried them—and Hallie would have heeded the instruction, even if Dair got tempted to play hero—but we'd gotten two full hours of rest.

Which was both a good thing and a bad thing. In truth, I actually didn't mind broken sleep, even when it meant I couldn't relax. Why didn't I mind? Because if my body was at peace during the night, my subconscious worked overtime, and then the nightmares came out to play. Sleepwalking was an occupational hazard. I'd seen too much, done too much, felt too much, and I relived the horrors in my dreams. And when one of my imaginary enemies attacked, I fought back in the real world.

It wasn't pretty.

But with a wild beast potentially lurking nearby, an inbuilt defence mechanism held the nightmares at bay, and I didn't unknowingly lash out at my nearest and dearest.

Danger for me meant safety for everyone else.

"Quiet as the grave," Dair said.

Nice choice of words. But I settled in with Sky and waited.

And waited.

And waited.

And...

"Do you feel that?"

"Feel what?" She looked up at the stars. "Is it raining?"

"Do you see any clouds?"

"No, but—"

"Shhh. Just...absorb."

For a full minute, she said nothing.

Then, "There's something out there."

"What do you feel?"

"I... I can't explain it. Just...something. Like a vibration in my spine, but barely a tingle."

Good. No, excellent. "Yup, there's something there, all right."

I studied the view through my goggles. Several white blobs moving slowly, mostly singles, but there was a cluster of a half-dozen life forms near the bottom of the slope. Those were definitely deer. What about higher up? Once I'd zoomed in to the first position, I switched to night vision for a clearer picture and saw another deer emerge from the trees.

"Look," Sky whispered. "To the south."

I panned left and saw two glowing orbs, greenish against the darkness, but when I flipped the goggles up, they shone red instead.

"Should we...?" Sky was already halfway up.

"Wait."

I flipped back to thermal. Interesting. There was no heat source around the orbs, nothing at all.

But when I panned farther back, I saw that where there'd previously been five lone white blobs moving across the slope above the deer cluster, now there were only four.

Where had the fifth gone?

And to echo Sky's question, what the hell was it?

11

PAIGE

"So, why an insect? Why didn't Gregor Samsa transform into, say, a mouse or a spider?"

The professor was speaking, but his words barely registered, and my copy of *The Metamorphosis* lay closed on the desk in front of me. I quickly covered my yawn with a hand. Last night, I'd spent nine hours lying in the most comfortable bed I'd ever known in my life, so why hadn't I been able to sleep?

You know why, Paige.

My life was out of control. My comfortable existence had turned into a Kafkaesque nightmare. The spiral into hell had started in the summer when I'd accidentally bought Glendoon Hall, and last week, I'd sidestepped into madness when I broke down on the man I'd had a secret, forbidden crush on for over a year. Then the whole world had taken a trip to Crazytown when Emmy Black walked into my life with Sky Malone and Hallie Chastain.

I'd resigned myself to being stuck in the stable at Glendoon for the foreseeable future. To living on a painfully tight budget for the rest of the school year, then flying home

77

to confess to my mom that I'd wasted all the money Grandma had left me.

But Fletcher wouldn't let up. When I hadn't answered his emails—because what was I meant to say?—he'd gotten more and more worried until he was ready to report me as missing if I didn't confirm I was okay. So I'd called and he'd pushed, pushed, pushed. Refused to accept my claim that I was fine and having a bonny old time here in Scotland. I'd chattered on for ten minutes about the countryside and the deer and the rabbits, and Fletcher had let me talk until I ran out of lies to tell. Then he'd held my gaze—I'd video-called because I was freezing and seeing his handsome face always sent a rush of warmth through me—and said that if I was truly happy, then I had to look him in the eye and tell him so.

And...I couldn't. Even thousands of miles apart, having barely spoken for months, we still had a connection. I'd felt it the moment I met him in Thailand, and now I wasn't sure I'd ever be able to sever that thread.

Nothing had happened in Thailand, of course, not in *that* way. I'd been with Jez back then, and I wasn't a cheater. The last night, I'd come close, but...no. No, I'd held firm. And Fletcher... He'd been unattainable. A unicorn. A mythical creature, so hard to find and impossible to catch. Amazingly kind, a great listener, smart, sexy, patient, compassionate... Way, way out of my league. And also about to move to Antarctica.

At that time, life had been mostly sunshine and roses with Jez. Well, lotuses and orchids and beautiful golden ratchaphruek trees. Thailand had been the adventure of a lifetime, two months spent volunteering as English teachers in a Thai school, with swimming, sunbathing, and sightseeing on the weekends. A summer of fun before he moved back to Scotland to finish his degree.

We'd plotted out our whole future together. Jez had an

entrepreneurial spirit. His plan had been to start his own business and become a digital nomad, for us to travel across the world after I'd graduated and see everything it had to offer. He'd suffered a setback when he lost most of his savings trading shares online, but he hadn't been worried. No, he'd actually been quite blasé. A temporary setback, failure is an integral part of success, yadda yadda yadda. He'd taken a job in an office as an interim measure while he came up with his next endeavour, and we'd agreed to share the profits from flipping the apartment we were meant to buy and put the money toward our dream.

But now? Now, I was kicking myself.

From every possible angle.

Oh, heck. I'd zoned out again and now the professor was asking the class a question. What did we, as readers, see as the most striking elements of Kafka's vision? At the moment, my brain was such a mush of confusion that I could barely name a single one of his stories beyond *The Metamorphosis*, let alone analyse his words.

What was that? We needed to write an essay on the subject? The paper was due in two weeks, which bought me time but also added an extra element of difficulty since I'd zoned out for the entire lecture. How had I ever thought that leaving the US, leaving everything I knew, would be a good idea?

For the tenth time today, I checked my phone. Nothing. What was going on at Glendoon? How much longer could I stay in the Caladar Hotel? Every time I walked past a member of staff there, my chest tightened as I waited for them to tell me there'd been a mistake, that I was responsible for the whole cost of my room and I needed to pay *right now*.

"Excuse me? Can I get past?"

"Uh..." Right, everyone was leaving. The lecture was over, and I hadn't even noticed. "Sorry, sure."

What now? Should I go back to the hotel? I hadn't seen Emmy for days. Last night, two girls my age who said they worked with her had come to my room to see if I wanted to go out for dinner, but I couldn't afford restaurant prices, so I'd made an excuse. Tired, needed to study, college in the morning. I was almost sure they'd believed me. Even if they hadn't, they'd wished me a pleasant evening and told me to enjoy the room service.

So I'd ordered another cheese-and-tomato pizza—the cheapest thing on the menu because I didn't want to take advantage of Emmy's generosity—then settled in for one more restless night.

And during the little sleep I got, I'd dreamed of Fletcher Braun.

Of warm sable eyes, of tousled hair the colour of teak, of the cute dimples he got when he smiled, which was often. We'd spent so many evenings sitting on the beach, just talking and listening to the waves. Watching the sunset. Fletcher had been in Thailand to volunteer at a turtle sanctuary, and his passion for the project had been contagious.

Jez? Well, he preferred to go out in the evenings, and I'd had no problem with that—he was an extrovert; I was an introvert. Yin and yang. Jez liked to play basketball and work out in the gym and go to clubs and sing karaoke while I was happier reading a book. Oh, we ventured out together a couple of times a week, and I enjoyed those excursions, but every day? No, that wasn't for me. I'd always thought we complemented each other, that the old adage "opposites attract" had been true, but now I realised our values had been as different as our personalities. I'd stuck by him when he lost his money, even sent him cash from my savings for rent, and then he'd skipped out on me when I made my own mistakes.

All those months I'd felt guilty for emailing Fletcher... Yet he was the man who'd come to my aid.

How could I thank him? I had no idea what to say, and considering my major was English Literature—with a name like Paige Turner, what else could it be?—that was a pretty poor state of affairs. I checked my phone again. No messages, not one. I hadn't heard from Fletcher since that tearful phone call, but he'd told me not to worry, that a storm was affecting communications in Antarctica, and he'd be fine.

I wanted to believe that.

Had to believe that.

I left the lecture theatre on autopilot. Should I head to the library? The Caladar? Glendoon Hall? Honestly, I never wanted to see that place again, but the not-knowing was eating away at me. I should speak with Emmy. Find out where I stood.

Nerves already shredded, I headed for my car.

12

EMMY

"Okay... Turn it on," Ross instructed.

Sky opened the tap in the stable yard, and water gushed over her feet as she leapt back. Halle-fucking-lujah. That almost made my visit to Ratmageddon in the cellar worth it, even if it had been something of a wasted trip. In the end, we'd located the internal stopcock on the far side of the house, in what had once been a laundry room. We'd found an additional back door too, so overgrown that it was all but invisible from outside. Another hour, and between the six of us—me, Sky, Ross, and his three buddies—we'd hacked away the bushes, and now we had a way in and out that didn't involve climbing through a window or playing Russian roulette with a rotten floor. The front door was still jammed solid, swollen shut by years of rain, and none of us wanted to force it open in case we couldn't close it again. That was a challenge for another day.

"Isn't this water kinda brown?" Sky asked.

"Aye, but that's to be expected when the taps haven't been run for years. There'll be sediment in the pipes. We'll try flushing the water through for twenty minutes, see where that gets us."

Hopefully, it wouldn't freeze tonight—otherwise we'd have a skating rink in the morning. The forecast said it should hover around one to two degrees Celsius, and there was good cloud cover, so maybe we'd be okay. And having water, that was a significant achievement. A better generator would be arriving tomorrow—one with a larger power capacity and, I was assured, improved reliability—and we could use that to light the place until Marc managed to rewire the mains supply. We'd found the fuse box during our hunt for the stopcock, an ancient cracked thing made of Bakelite with loose wires hanging out like deadly spaghetti. More than once, I'd been accused of having a death wish, but not even I would risk flipping a switch on that thing.

There was still a ton of work to be done, but we had water, and we had a plan. Tomorrow, Marc would start on the electrics while the rest of us played hunt-the-septic-tank. And once we'd found it, we could go mobile-home shopping. By that point, Bradley would surely have provided some guidance. I'd sent him an email outlining the situation, but he'd been quiet over the last few days. Perhaps I should have been grateful for the peace, but the radio silence had me worried.

Very worried.

"Surprise!"

I whirled to find Fletcher standing beside our borrowed SUV—one of the Blackwood pool cars—and he wasn't alone. No, Nick was with him. Aw, they'd come to visit? That was—

Wait a second... *Why* was Nick with him?

"What the hell are you doing here?"

"Do I need a reason to come see my favourite ex-girlfriend?"

He leaned down to kiss me on the cheek, ignoring my narrowed eyes.

"When she's on a different continent? Yes."

"I figured I'd give Fletch some moral support with... whatever it is he's doing. And I haven't visited the Edinburgh field office in years."

"Exactly, because the Edinburgh field office runs just fine on its own. And didn't you trust me to have everything under control here?"

"Of course, babe."

"Then why are you here?"

"So..." Nick fidgeted with his jacket collar. "So Bradley thought it would be cute to get some turkeys for Thanksgiving."

Okay, now we were getting to the bottom of this.

"Isn't that what he usually does?"

"*Live* turkeys. For *ambience*. They arrived last night, and he swears he ordered ten, but somewhere along the line, a decimal point got misplaced."

Shit.

"So now we have a hundred live turkeys? At Riverley? Tell me they're in a cage."

"They *were* in a cage. Seems the catch was faulty. When Bradley got back from New York, they were running around all over the place. Guess Thanksgiving's gonna be a real turkey shoot."

Fuck my damn life. "Is Black still in LA? Because I can see it turning into a Bradley shoot."

"I gave Black a heads-up and suggested he might want to stay on the West Coast. Nate's allegedly flown to Cuba to visit a third cousin I'm pretty sure doesn't exist, and Carmen's cleaning her guns."

"Where's Lara? You didn't leave her behind, did you?"

"She's jet-lagged, so she decided to check out the spa at the hotel and then take a nap."

"Well, in that case..." I waved a hand in the general direction of the house. "Welcome to the fun factory."

Fletcher took a look around and gave a low whistle. "Paige bought this?"

"Unfortunately."

"She said it was a real mess, but...sheesh. Do *any* of the windows have glass in them?"

"Possibly, but those ones are hidden by ivy. Be careful if you go inside—there's a bloody great hole in the floor."

He shook his head, incredulous. "Where *is* Paige?"

"You didn't call her?"

He shared a glance with Nick. "Thought I'd surprise her."

"She's at the university. Or maybe back at the hotel by now."

Or not.

A moment later, Paige's hatchback nosed around the corner of the building, and I watched her carefully as she spotted Fletcher. Her jaw dropped. Shock crossed her face, followed by something softer. Then she hit the gas instead of the brakes and crashed into my SUV.

For the love of...

As the *crack* of breaking plastic echoed around the stable yard, Paige covered her face with her hands and burst into tears.

I looked at Nick and Nick looked at me. Behind him, Sky was trying not to laugh.

This week really had been sent to try us.

Marc stuck his head out of the laundry room door. "What happened?"

"Fender bender."

Fletcher was already running towards Paige's car. Ah, so sweet.

85

"Has he got this handled?" I asked Nick.

"Probably." He turned his attention to the house. "So, what's the story? There's water now?"

"As of five minutes ago, yes."

I caught Nick up on the events of the past twenty-four hours—the building progress plus our nocturnal shenanigans as we tried to solve the mystery of what was lurking in the forest behind Glendoon Hall. Last night's sound-and-light show was a puzzle.

"Dogs howl," he said. "One of our neighbours has a Labrador and Lara swears it's part werewolf."

"*Could* be a dog making the noise. And given an appropriate light source reflecting on the tapetum lucidum, the red eyes could have been an owl, outside chance of a fox."

"Why an outside chance?"

"They were too high up. A fox would've been hidden by the undergrowth."

"So, what's your gut feeling?" he asked. "It's some kind of animal?"

"No, because there *was* no obvious light source to cause a reflection. The moon was dropping behind the hill, and there's no mains electricity."

"A flashlight?"

I clapped Nick's cheeks between my palms. "Bingo. And who has the opposable thumbs to work a flashlight?"

"A person?"

"No flies on you, Sherlock."

"Why would a person be up on the hill?"

"That, Nicky, is the sixty-four-thousand-dollar question. I can think of three reasons—kids messing around, a local looking to boost tourism, or something more sinister."

Sky joined us. "Or option four—the Beast of Glendoon exists. We found giant paw prints."

I wasn't going to dignify that suggestion with a response.

"And do you know the interesting thing? The so-called eyes glowed in the same place two nights running, at the same time to the minute. Almost as if they were..."

"On a timer," Nick finished, and Sky's expression turned sulky.

I gave her a nudge. "Cheer up, brat. We'll catch your beast, except it'll be the two-legged kind rather than four-legged."

"Whatever."

I used the term "beast" as a joke. But if I'd realised just what a monster we were really after, I'd have sharpened my damn claws first.

13

PAIGE

Fletcher filled the driver's side of the car as he leaned over me, biceps bulging an inch from my nose.

"Let's put the parking brake on, all right?"

"Yes," I whispered. What else could I say?

My cheeks burned with shame. I'd always been a klutz, but these past six months, it was as if I'd supercharged my clumsiness. And now I'd come to speak with the woman who'd gone out of her way to help me—without even *knowing* me—and I'd driven into her car.

"I'm so sorry."

"Are you okay?"

"Just mortally embarrassed." I couldn't even face him. "How bad is the damage?"

"Nothing serious."

"Did you even look?"

"There's no need. If you're okay, then it's nothing serious."

"But Emmy's car..."

"I'm not real tight with Emmy, but from what I've heard, she can afford a new bumper."

Fletcher settled onto the door sill, trapping me where I sat, his arm a fraction of an inch from my thigh but not actually touching. I had to take comfort in the familiar. In all of our sunset chats, he'd only ever touched me once.

On that final night.

Our goodbye.

We'd met in our favourite spot, a flat rock beneath a small clump of palm trees. When we sat on the edge, we could dangle our feet in the sea and let the azure water lap around our ankles. I used to be scared of the sea. Not the water itself, but what lay underneath it. Then Fletcher had convinced me to give snorkelling a try, and I'd realised that beauty lurked beneath the waves, not beasts.

He'd taught me how to be brave.

Sadly, he hadn't taught me how to be smart as well.

But that evening, a year before I'd ever heard of Glendoon, we'd spoken of our hopes for the future. I wanted to write a bestselling novel. He wanted to discover the secrets of the world we lived in, and I had no doubt that he would. He'd wrapped his arms around me, held me as we watched the sun dip below the horizon in a blaze of pinks and oranges. And then...our gazes met. I'd come within a hair's breadth of kissing him, my heart thudding against my ribcage and his beating in unison.

But then my watch had beeped, reminding me I was meant to be meeting Jez for dinner at the Seashell Bar in fifteen minutes, and *he* was the man I shared my bed with, not Fletcher Braun. Treat others as I'd want to be treated myself, that's what Mom had always told me, and I couldn't— wouldn't—cheat on my boyfriend.

So I'd run. I'd run right out of Fletcher's life, quite literally. I still had the scar from the steps I'd tripped up in my haste, and instead of eating noodles in the Seashell Bar, I'd spent the evening in the emergency room getting eight stitches in my knee. Jez hadn't left my side the whole time, hadn't even changed out of his basketball shorts, and I thought I'd made the right choice.

I'd been wrong.

Even before the Glendoon disaster, I'd had regrets about my decision. *If one good deed in all my life I did, I do repent it from my very soul.* But I couldn't turn back the clock.

At least, I'd always thought so.

But now Fletcher was right here, sitting next to me, invading my space with muscles and pheromones and soft, kind words, and he looked so good. Sounded so good. Smelled so good, like cedar and old leather and—

Wait. Was I actually sniffing his freaking hair? Because no, no, no, that was a really bad idea.

"I've messed everything up," I whispered.

"Not everything. And nobody gets through life without making a few mistakes."

"I bet you don't make mistakes. Or Emmy."

"Once upon a time when I was at college, I left a UV light on, which was a definite mistake because those can melt everything. Then, in the middle of the night, I suddenly realised what I'd done and ran back to the lab, but I didn't know there was a silent alarm, which meant I had to explain to campus security why I was stumbling around in my pyjamas."

I swallowed a giggle. "Did anything melt?"

"I got lucky and the bulb burned out first. And Emmy managed to break my brother's nose in her sleep, so no, you're not the only person who makes mistakes." She *broke* his *nose*? And they were still talking? Fletcher squeezed my hand, and a bolt of electricity shot up my arm. "You've just been unlucky, that's all."

"Maybe..." My voice came out as a croak, and I tried again. "Maybe my luck's changing."

"That's for sure. Your faucet is working now."

"What? There's water? Where?"

Fletcher rose to his feet and offered a hand. I stared for a moment. This...this was new. But I liked it. I put my hand in his and climbed out of the car, or at least I tried to, but I was still wearing my seat belt so I didn't get very far. Dammit!

"Don't stress, just relax. Take things slowly."

I tried again, and this time, I managed to leave the vehicle successfully. A small win, but I'd take it.

And wow, there *was* water. It cascaded out of the faucet on the old carriage house and flowed across the cobbles. Beautiful, clear water, a sight more glorious than the purest mountain stream. Even if it wasn't drinkable, I could still use it to wash dishes. Wash my underwear. Heck, I could rig up a shower and use it to wash myself in the warmer months.

"I... I... Just thank you. *Thank you.*"

Emmy grinned. "Today water, tomorrow electricity, next week the world."

"Electricity? You don't have to—"

"Yeah, we do."

"I'm so sorry about your car. Honestly, I don't know what happened."

"Eh, it's only a bumper. Have you eaten lunch?"

"No, I—"

"Fletcher, why don't you take Paige out for a late lunch? The Glendoon Inn does decent food."

"That's nearby?" he asked.

"Turn left out of the gates, and it's a quarter-mile on the right. Bring me back a sandwich? I'm bloody starving. Sky, you want something?"

"A cheese-and-pickle roll with salt-and-vinegar crisps. The guys brought lunch, but Nick's probably hungry."

Emmy and Sky were just so *casual* about everything. So... so unbothered. I aspired to that level of zen, but I was quite certain I'd never reach it.

Fletcher's thumb stroked over my knuckles, and I jolted.

"Lunch?" he asked.

"Uh, okay."

"I can't believe you came here."

"Why?"

The cosy table in a quiet corner of the Glendoon Inn gave Fletcher and me the privacy we needed to talk, but once again, I found that I had no idea what to say.

"Because... Because you live on the other side of the world."

"And when a friend's in trouble, I'm gonna help."

Friends. Right. He'd said that in his first email from Antarctica. I'd read it a hundred times. A thousand. *I've never been good with words, but I don't want to leave the deep freeze in a year and find that all my friends have forgotten me. So here's a cute picture of a humpback whale.*

I'd laughed because the whale was as uncute as an animal could get and also with relief because I'd been so sure that I'd never hear from Fletcher again, not after the way I'd run out on him. Now he'd offered me a lifeline, and I grabbed it with both hands. Well, kind of. What I actually did was text him a picture in return. Finding an actual whale was out of the question, so I'd swallowed the lump in my throat and hurried over to the library to snap a photo of *Moby Dick*.

Me: Sorry, this is the best I can do.

And then we'd carried on writing to each other, fallen back into the same easy conversation we'd started in Thailand. Fletcher had given me a virtual tour of Antarctica, and I'd followed his lead and learned to love the nature on my doorstep with weekend trips to the park and the beach. Until I met him, I'd always been more of an indoor person, but he'd taught me there was a whole other part of the world just waiting to be explored. Even Glendoon had a macabre beauty, and I'd spotted badgers and barn owls, hedgehogs and hen harriers, pine martens and peregrine falcons, red deer and ravens...

But then I'd ghosted Fletcher. I'd screwed up, I'd shut down, and I'd pushed him away.

Now he was here.

And I was at an absolute loss for words.

"So..." I began, trying desperately to keep my tears in check. "Welcome to Scotland."

"How's college going?"

"Uh, okay, I think?" *Stay positive, Paige.* "I mean, I get tired a lot, but since I have zero social life, I've been able to spend plenty of time on my assignments."

"Know that feeling. The past year, I've spent more time with penguins than I have with people."

Relief trickled through my veins. This...this was more like the old days. Just the two of us talking, no pressure.

"The project's wrapped up now?"

"Yeah, we obtained some good data, and I have a thousand more pictures to show you. Right before I left, a pod of orcas was playing in front of the research station, so there's video too."

"I can't wait to see that. I managed to film a red squirrel at Glendoon last week, or maybe the week before. It sat on the seat of the old tractor as if it was driving the thing."

Aileen appeared, order book in hand. "What can I get for you both?"

For me, that was an easy question. "A bowl of soup, please."

She gave me a wink. "I'll bring extra bread. I hear there's work going on at Glendoon Hall?"

"Only for a day or two. I have water now."

Her smile was genuine. Out of all the people in the village, Aileen had been the kindest. If there were leftovers, she'd save them for me, plus she kept crusts that I could feed to the birds even though she didn't have much money herself. Times were hard. Her husband had lost his job earlier in the year when his employer sold out to a venture capitalist, and there wasn't much work available around here.

Fletcher made his own choice—a club sandwich—then rattled off orders for Emmy, Sky, and Nick. As Aileen swished off back to the bar, he reached across the table and took my hand in his. The questions were about to get harder.

"So, what happened this summer? Not the condensed version you gave me before. Everything."

I owed him that much. Right now, I owed him my sanity. So I started at the beginning with Grandma Charlotte's passing, cringed inwardly as I told him about the auction, the fight with Jez, the horror when I arrived at Glendoon. My difficulties with surviving in a home with no utilities an hour from college and my despair that I'd ruined my future with one stupid mistake.

And at the end, Fletcher wiped my tears away with a napkin and cupped my cheeks in his hands.

"You might have made a mistake, but Jez made a bigger one."

"I still can't believe he ditched me like that. With a freaking phone call."

"I can. The man was a fool in every way. He paid more attention to his workouts than he did to you, and he always thought he knew better than everyone around him, which is why he asked for vagina water every time he went to a restaurant instead of dipping sauce, and also why he was convinced he could make a fortune by fucking around on the internet instead of working."

"He lost all his savings."

"And then he encouraged you to lose yours as well."

"He said property was the safest investment, better than leaving my money in a bank."

"He lied."

And I'd believed him, so who was the bigger fool in the end?

"The vagina water thing? Is that true?"

I thought some of the waitstaff had looked at him funny.

"Yeah, it's true. One of my Thai friends had a sister who worked at the Seashell Bar, and she tried to correct him, but he told her she was wrong. The guy's a jackass. A self-centred jackass. And let's put it this way... If I were him, I wouldn't have let my girl spend every damn evening with a man like me."

"Why?"

"Because, dear Paige..." Fletcher's lips curved into a wolfish grin. "Now I have you, and he doesn't. And I'm keeping you."

What?

Oh my.

14

EMMY

My phone pinged with an email, not my work phone but my personal phone, the one hardly anyone had the number for. *Why hello, Mr. President.* I put down the machete I was using to hack at a clump of brambles and read what he had to say.

James: Is this a joke?

I clicked on the attachment and found an email. To James. From Bradley. What the fuck? I hit dial. Waited.

"Hey, *chica linda*," James murmured, his voice soft. Warm.

An old nickname, but I'd known James for a long time. Black had known him for even longer. They'd gone to school together, been best friends until I fucked up and made things awkward between them. Slowly, slowly, things were getting better, but there was still a ways to go.

"I'm going to kill him."

"Who, Bradley?" James asked.

"Who else?"

"The turkey offer—is it genuine?"

"In the absence of further information, I'm gonna go with 'yes.' Last I heard, there were a hundred turkeys running loose around Riverley and Carmen had been tasked with fixing the problem."

"You're not at home?"

"Are you kidding me? I'm not spending Thanksgiving cleaning up turkey shit. No, I'm in Scotland."

"Why Scotland?"

"Long story. By night, I'm hunting for a mysterious beast with the body of a wolf and the wings of an eagle, and by day, I'm hunting for a septic tank."

"Is that safe?"

"I've already been scratched to fuck by brambles, and Sky nearly took my head off with an axe, so no. Plus septic tanks can give off noxious fumes, so let's hope I don't fall into the damn thing."

"I meant the beast-hunting."

"Oh, that part'll be fine. So, the turkeys..."

"We already have two birds for the pardoning ceremony. Wishbone and Turkey McTurkeyface." I heard the smile in his voice. "They're out in an enclosure by the tennis pavilion."

I suppose I had to give Bradley a smidgen of credit for getting creative in his turkey disposal attempts. A lesser man would have called up the nearest slaughterhouse, not tried to offload a pair onto the President of the United States.

"Turkey McTurkeyface? Who picked the names?"

"A public vote on the White House website."

"What were the runners-up?"

"I believe those were Drumstick and Bullseye."

"So how about this... You pardon two extra turkeys, and the people who voted for Drumstick and Bullseye will be happy. The animal-rights people will be happy. The turkeys will be happy. And I'll be fucking thrilled because then I'll

97

only have ninety-eight turkeys running around my yard instead of the full ton."

"Tradition dictates that I pardon one turkey."

"Dude, the guy before you served the turkeys McNugget-style to the Japanese ambassador's vegan wife. I think you can get away with pardoning a couple of extra birds."

In the silence that followed, I pictured James running a hand through his hair. Perhaps muttering a few oaths at the ceiling the way he did when he was exasperated. But finally, he acquiesced.

"If Bradley can get the turkeys here by seven a.m. tomorrow morning, I'll do it. No later. I have to fly to an energy summit in Ireland right after the photo op."

"Aw, for that I'll bring you a haggis."

"Tell me I don't need to pardon the haggis as well?"

"No, and to be fair, you probably wouldn't want to eat it either. How about a tin of shortbread instead?"

"Talk to you soon, Linny."

"Laters."

Two down, ninety-eight to go. Maybe Kitty could help? My oversized cat, also known as the Beast of Riverley? He'd tried to eat a parrot not so long ago, so he definitely had a taste for feathers. And speaking of food, where was my bloody sandwich? Fletcher had left for the Glendoon Inn an hour ago, and the service was pretty quick there. Once I'd eaten, I planned to take another walk up the hill.

I had a theory, and I wanted to see if it panned out.

"Those prints weren't made by a wolf."

Fletcher studied the photos on my phone, then put it back

on the table as I took another bite of egg mayo on rye. When he arrived back with Paige, he'd opened her car door, then taken her hand as they walked to the stable. He hadn't let go of it since.

Earlier, Nick had bet me five bucks that the two of them would be an item by the end of the week, and I'd taken that bet because Paige struck me as a cautious type of girl. But I'd stupidly forgotten the power of the Goldman-Braun aura— even with my self-control, I'd only lasted three weeks between meeting Nick and ending up underneath him—and now I was going to lose.

But who cared? They seemed happy.

Sky, on the other hand, wasn't.

"How can you be sure a wolf didn't make them? They're way bigger than dog paws."

"Because three years ago, I spent a month in Alaska studying the hunting behaviour of grey wolves, and that's not how they move." Fletcher picked up the phone again and zoomed in. "Take a look at this track—not the individual prints, the whole track. When a wolf walks, more of their weight goes to their front limbs than their hinds, so the front paws sort of...splay out. The overall shape is quite round. The hind paws, they take less of the weight, so they end up oval. If you look at a wolf track, you'd expect to see round, round, oval, oval, round, round, oval, oval, and so on. These are all round."

Interesting.

"So what did make the prints, Richard Attenborough?" Sky asked.

"*David* Attenborough. Richard was an actor, David was the nature guy."

"Okay, fine. What made the prints?"

"I don't know. I can only tell you what didn't make them.

But if I had to guess, I'd say a person pretending to be a wolf. They're so uniform."

Even more interesting.

"Why would somebody do that?" Sky asked.

"I'm a zoologist, not a detective." Fletcher shrugged. "Are there any more chips?"

A howl came from my left.

Close.

Too close.

Chills ran down my spine, but the animal's cry wasn't what spooked me the most. No, I was more concerned that my sixth sense hadn't clued me in to a potential predator nearby.

I'd felt nothing.

Not a twitch, not a tingle.

Nick was twenty yards behind me, Sky another twenty behind him. Ross had offered to come as well, but since I was carrying a gun I wasn't meant to have, I'd declined. It was just the three of us.

I motioned Nick forward, noting the slight hint of puzzlement on his face. He felt it too. Or rather, he didn't feel it.

There. The howl came again, and this time I got no chills, only a warm glow of satisfaction. I'd been right.

Nick was already studying the branches above my head when I reached his side, and now Sky was the one who looked confused.

Ah, there it was.

"Gimme a boost?"

Nick crouched so I could sit on his shoulders, and when he stood again, my head was level with the motion sensor screwed to the trunk of the tree. When I followed the wires, I found a plastic box in a hollow. A moment later, and with thanks to my handy multitool, I had the whole lot in my hands.

"What's that?" Sky asked.

"Your beast." I waved my hand in front of the sensor, and the howl sounded again. "That's fifty quid you owe me."

"You're kidding?"

"Nope. Pay up. And another fifty says that when we poke around a hundred yards in that direction"—I pointed up the slope—"we'll find a little plastic box with two red LEDs and a timer set to activate them at a quarter to six each morning."

"No way I'm taking that bet."

The box contained a small speaker arrangement, a PCB, and a pair of batteries—enough to power the contraption for several weeks at a guess. Our culprit would just have to check on the equipment once a month or so, and anyone venturing up onto the hill in the meantime would receive a good scare.

But if my sixth sense had been firing on all cylinders, he— or she—had been there last night and the night before.

Why?

The first visit could have been a regular battery change, but why risk coming for a second time so soon afterwards?

Was the increased activity around Glendoon Hall making our "beast" nervous?

It was possible.

That made me rule out kids—they wouldn't much care about being rumbled. *Ha-ha, good joke guys, let's go share a pack of ciggies behind the bus shelter.* No, our culprit had a stake in keeping rumours of the Beast of Glendoon's existence alive. That meant they wouldn't want a bunch of strangers hanging around Glendoon Hall. They wouldn't want any restoration work to happen, no electricity to shine a light on their night-time activities. And they certainly wouldn't want Paige living there for the next eight months.

All of which made them potentially dangerous.

Maybe Sky had been right?

Maybe there was a monster lurking in the forest after all?

15

HALLIE

M aeve's dad had run out on his family three years ago, and two years ago, her mom had been rushed into hospital with a perforated gallbladder. Dair offered to look after Maeve while his aunt recovered from surgery, and Maeve had hung out in the office each day after school until he finished work, just a temporary arrangement, or so everyone thought. When her mom came back home, Maeve still kept showing up.

Now she had a little desk in the corner of the Investigations section, and there was always someone around to assist with her homework. She also liked to help out by formatting reports and franking the mail, and when she proved reliable, Blackwood had made it official and started paying her to work for five hours per week.

And yesterday afternoon, Maeve had skipped into the office after school and proudly presented us with a chewed pen cap in a ziplock bag. Clare Muir's, she said, and she'd picked it up with a clean tissue to minimise contamination.

Emmy had been absolutely right about her.

But if I was interpreting the information in front of me correctly, then Maeve's most recent effort had been in vain.

I needed to call Valerie.

"Jake Burns, is he...?" I blurted when she answered.

"Our suspect's son? With ninety-nine percent probability, yes."

When I first started working at Blackwood, Dan had warned me that the job was a mixture of hard slog and what-the-fuck with small moments of elation. This was one of those moments. Billions of people on the planet, and we'd found our needle in the haystack.

But now we had to prove it, and also find out what had happened to Mila Carmody.

Her family needed closure.

"Are you still there?" Valerie asked.

"Just preparing to bow down at your feet."

She laughed her tinkly laugh. "Makes a change from the bread-and-butter ancestry research."

"Thank you, thank you, thank you."

We had him. With ninety-nine percent certainty, we had him. No need to collect the remaining sample, no more wasted time.

When Dair walked in with two giant mugs of coffee, I must have had the dumbest grin on my face.

"What happened? Did your fella call again?"

"No, it's Burns."

"Burns called? Jake Burns?"

Start at the beginning, Hallie. "No, Valerie emailed me. The genealogist. The first samples have been processed, and Jake Burns is the son of the man we're looking for."

"She's certain of that?"

"As certain as she can be. But I think we should try to get a sample from Jake's father to confirm."

"Agreed. Guess we'll be spending the morning on research, then." Indeed we would. "Let's find out where he lives."

As always, we started with the basics. Gordon Burns was fifty-eight years old, and his listed address was the same as his son's, a reasonably large bungalow on the outskirts of Bonnyrigg.

Burns senior had an average credit rating but little debt, just a Barclaycard with a small balance. No loans, no mortgage, no car payment. No social media other than a LinkedIn profile, which showed he'd worked as a customer services manager at a bank in Edinburgh before he quit six years ago. No occupation had been listed since. Had he retired early?

My phone rang, and my heart did that little skip it always did when I saw Ford's name flash up. Maybe the novelty would wear off at some point, but for now, I relished the buzz. And perhaps I was the tiniest bit homesick. This was the farthest I'd ever travelled, and although I was with friends, a part of me missed sleeping in my own bed at night.

"Hey, wait a second while I find somewhere quiet." A small meeting room lay empty, and I figured nobody would mind if I borrowed it for a moment. On screen, Ford's hair was mussed, and I recognised the old T-shirt as one he often slept in. "Did you just wake up?"

"Yeah." His voice was still husky. "And I miss seeing your face in the mornings, so..."

So the first thing he'd done was to call me. "I love you."

"Love you too, plum. You at work?"

"In the Edinburgh office." The picture moved, and I saw a familiar nightstand. "Are you in my apartment? I thought you were staying on the boat this week?"

"Mercy wanted to take an overnight trip with Cora and Lee— something about a project for the Blackwood Foundation—and she asked if I'd keep the parrot company. You want to say hello?"

"Sure."

The picture wobbled as he headed into the living room. Pinchy was in his cage, and when he saw Ford—aka food source—he began clawing his way up the bars and cursing. For a bird, he had a good vocabulary, but most of it consisted of the profanities a previous owner had taught him.

"Snack? Asshole."

Ford tipped pellets into Pinchy's dish, but he ignored them. Healthy food wasn't his favourite; he wanted fruit, and preferably mango.

Luckily, Ford was well-trained. "Okay, okay, give me a minute."

"Snack? Shit, shit. Don't shoot Mike."

Ah, yes. The "Mike" mystery. That was another problem to look into, but right now, we'd pushed it farther down the list. Until recently, we'd assumed Pinchy was telling us not to shoot a guy named Mike, and we'd even tried searching for gunshot victims with that name, but Bradley had come up with a different theory. Pinchy wasn't so good with punctuation, so maybe he was saying, "Don't shoot, Mike," instead? When I had space to breathe, I planned to look into shootings where the suspect was called Mike rather than the victim. Not that I wanted to return Pinchy to a former owner, but... I was curious. It was a loose end. And if Pinchy lived for another thirty years, which was a possibility, the not-knowing would forever bug me.

Ford opened the cage door, and Pinchy flew laps around the living room while Ford headed to the kitchen. *Love me, love my parrot.*

"How's the case going?" he asked.

"Better than I hoped." I caught Ford up on our recent DNA discovery. "If we can get that sample today, then there's a chance I can fly home in time for Thanksgiving." Why did he grimace? "What's wrong?"

"Much as I'd love to see you, if you have the option to stay in the UK for a few more days, I suggest you take it."

"What happened?"

"Turkeys happened."

"You're gonna have to explain."

So he did. Riverley was besieged. Bradley was freaking out. Carmen had offered to take care of the problem, but Bradley hated blood, so she was restricted to some kind of dart gun. Slater was helping, and Ford suspected that the loose turkeys were the real reason Cora, Lee, and Mercy had fled the state. Black was hiding out in California, Rafael had disappeared, Dan's kids had developed mysterious fevers, and Mack insisted she had to stay in the office to mind the place in everybody else's absence.

"Uh, so in that case, maybe I could stretch things out here a little longer. You don't mind?"

"We can hold our own Thanksgiving later, just the two of us. I'm planning on getting called into the office on Thursday —there's gonna be a murder."

"Bradley's?"

"If he doesn't catch those turkeys, I'd say it's a distinct possibility." Squawking sounded in the background. "I'm being summoned. Somebody wants more breakfast."

"Thanks for looking after him."

"Anytime, plum. Stay safe."

When I opened the meeting room door, I found Dair waiting for me, his mouth set into a thin line, and all the earlier triumph vanished. Uh-oh.

"Is there a problem?"

"Yeah, there's a problem. Gordon Burns isn't our guy."

"How do you know? We haven't even spoken with him."

He crooked a finger, and I followed him to his laptop. On the screen was a fundraising page, the Burns family asking for donations to adapt their home for a wheelchair following their beloved father's stroke. I checked the date. Six years ago. Six years ago, Gordon Burns had been in a wheelchair, and unless he'd made a miraculous recovery, there was no way he could have climbed through Mila Carmody's bedroom window and spirited her away to a destination unknown.

"So what are you saying? That Gordon Burns isn't Jake's father?"

"I'm saying that it's unlikely Gordon Burns could have left the blood on that little girl's window latch. Is he Jake's father?" Dair scrolled down the page. "There's a definite family resemblance, don't you think? And your genealogist believes our suspect is a member of the Burns family."

This got messier and messier... "Maybe Jake's mom had an affair? With a relative of Gordon's? Does he have any brothers?"

"Two brothers."

Terrific—one sample had just become three. And if one of those samples matched our suspect in the Carmody case, we were about to tear the Burns family apart in every possible way.

16

EMMY

"Well, that's perfectly gross."

Sky peered into the hole beside me, and she wasn't wrong. The septic tank had been covered by a rusting metal cover, and when we dragged it to the side, we'd found ourselves looking into a sea of fetid brown scum.

Marry a billionaire, they said. Your life'll be glitz and glamour, they said.

They lied.

"Good thing I've got a strong stomach."

"How deep do you think it is?"

"Pretty deep."

The scum came to within a foot of the lid, but how far down was the bottom? When we got the thing emptied, would we need a big tanker or a *really* big tanker? Ross had said that after we'd had the sludge sucked out, if the walls were intact, we could try rehabilitating the drainage field by flushing the pipes through and adding appropriate bacteria. It wouldn't be as good as a more modern system, but with any luck, it would be adequate for Paige and potentially Fletcher.

Nick picked up a nearby branch and snapped off most of the twiggy bits. "Try using this to gauge the depth."

"Why don't *you* try it?"

"Because this is your show. I'm only here because Lara's gone to the spa."

So he said, but he wasn't telling the whole truth. He wanted to help Paige because there was a good chance she'd become his future sister-in-law if the looks Fletcher had been giving her over dinner last night were any indication.

Ah, speaking of the wannabe knight in shining armour, here he was.

"Hey, you found the septic tank?"

"Emmy's just going to see how deep it is," Nick told his brother.

Fine. Fine, I'd do it. Then I was heading to the Glendoon Inn to catch up on sleep. I'd spent half of last night watching the hill out back, but our nocturnal visitor had been conspicuous by their absence. The red lights had blinked on at a quarter to six, though. It was so satisfying to be right.

The branch Nick handed me was a sturdy specimen, an inch and a half in diameter and at least five feet long. Would that be enough? I stuck it through the layer of scum and felt lumps, but it didn't hit the bottom. Yeah, we were gonna need the mother of all pumping trucks. How long would that take to arrange? If we could get it done this week, and Marc could sort out some basic wiring, then we'd just have to find a mobile home. Maybe I could delegate that part to Bradley after he'd finished up with the turkeys? It was basically shopping. He loved shopping.

I gave the branch one last jiggle and brought it up, complete with a skull lodged on the end.

A *human* skull.

Ah.

Fuck.

"Is that...?" Sky asked, eyes wide.

"How about we just put it back and pretend we didn't see it?"

"Emmy..." Nick warned.

"Okay, okay, fine."

I moved slowly, careful not to dislodge the skull as I lifted it through the hatch. The branch was wedged into an eye socket, and the smell that followed it up was vile.

Sky gagged.

"Don't puke at a crime scene."

"When I was younger, I thought it would be cool to be one of those CSI people in the little paper suits. Now I've changed my mind."

Understandable. Emptying out the tank and identifying the person entombed within it sure would present an interesting challenge.

As would catching whoever put them there.

Or would it?

"Och, that's reekie. You found the—" Ross started, appearing from the direction of the stable yard. "Fuck me, is that...?"

"It was in the septic tank."

He leaned forward for a closer look, then quickly thought better. "Where's the rest of it?"

"Probably floating in six feet of sewage." I offered him the branch. "Want to take a look?"

"No, yer all right. Have you called the police?"

"Not yet."

Ross pulled out his phone. "Then I should—"

"Wait." I held up a hand. "Just wait a second."

What did we have? At this semi-derelict mini-castle that clung to the edge of the wilderness, what did we have? I put down the branch and began pacing. I always thought better when I was moving—something about the repetitive motion made my synapses fire.

"I'm gonna go out on a limb here and say that whoever this skull once belonged to didn't voluntarily take a swim in a septic tank." Kids did stupid things for dares, but there was stupid and there was downright disgusting. "So we've probably got a murder victim."

Ross nodded. "Aye, that's a fair bet."

"We've got an abandoned property that hasn't been inhabited for decades. Long enough that someone probably thought it would crumble into ruin and the grounds were a safe place to dump a body."

"True enough."

"Locals don't come near the place because an enterprising soul started rumours of a Scottish Chimera running around the hills beyond, rumours fuelled by the local tourist industry because they've got to make money somehow, don't they? Years passed—and I suspect it was years because the body's nothing but bones in a closed tank with no access for scavengers—and the perp thought he'd gotten away with it. Brambles grew across the hatch. The house rotted. Who would ever stumble across this hiding place? And then Paige fucked up and moved in. Suddenly, our man—and let's assume it *is* a man because statistically, that's likely to be the case—has a problem."

Easy enough to slide a body into a septic tank, not so straightforward to get it out again, especially if it was in pieces. He couldn't move it. And if we tried emptying the tank, there'd probably be some sort of filter on the pump, and the bones would get stuck, and *gotcha*. He'd be found out. I stared up at the hill for a moment. Red eyes. Eerie howls. All those heat signatures...

"He spies on Paige. Waits. Breathes a little easier when he realises she's only camping out, not disturbing anything.

Perhaps he hears the stories in the village—some dumb American girl bought the place by accident, and she can't wait to move out. But he adds a few safeguards, just in case. Little widgets in the woods to scare people away. Makes himself a pair of giant wolf paws so he can meander through the trees from time to time. He could've cast them out of concrete, carved them out of wood..."

"3D printed them," Sky suggested. "You're so last century."

Thanks for the reminder, kid.

"Yes, or 3D printed them. And it works. He starts to feel comfortable again. Paige doesn't venture out, hell, she's hardly ever there. But then *we* arrive, and now he's *really* nervous. Who are we? Why are we here? We're rigging up lights, we're in the house, we're clearing ivy... He's watching. He's been up there in the early hours, trying to work out what the fuck's going on. Panicking. Wondering how close we are to discovering his secret." Finally, I grinned. "Bet you a fiver he's up there again tonight."

Sky glanced at the skull again. "Playing devil's advocate, what if the stalker in the woods is just some dude from the local gift shop trying to drum up business?"

"That's possible," I admitted. "Unlikely, since he's been there two mornings running and who would get up that early for fun, but possible. Don't you want to find out for sure?"

"Okay, I'll bite. How?"

To channel Bradley: duh. "By catching him. We've got four Royal Marines, a Navy SEAL, two investigators, and us. I'm sure we can manage an itty-bitty stake-out."

"What about the police?" Ross asked. "There's a dead body here."

"A day or two's delay won't make much difference, not after all this time. And if my theory's correct, that delay could allow the cops to solve the case a hell of a lot faster. I'll take full responsibility for the decision."

"Couldn't the police do their own stake-out?"

"They could, but you know damn well they'll turn up in marked cars and put up a crime scene tent and have CSIs crawling in every nook and cranny first because that's how they work. And the perp'll quietly retreat, melt into his hole and hope nobody looks for him there. And maybe they will, maybe they won't. Most of the evidence is gone now."

"I guess I can understand where you're coming from, but I can't just agree. I'll have to speak with the others first. We're all involved now."

"Fair enough. But in the meantime, we need to find a container for this skull, and then we should cover up the septic tank so it looks as if we haven't found it. Sky, grab the other side of that lid."

Half an hour later, we'd rearranged the brambles, and there were so many of them, you'd never know we'd found the tank. A pair of leather gloves I'd borrowed from Griff had protected me from the worst of the scratches, but I'd torn my jacket and several of the thorns had made it through my jeans.

Nick tipped Paige's ramen out of a storage box and sanitised it, and we stowed the skull safely inside. Thankfully, he'd also found a small pot of Vicks in her first aid kit and I'd smeared it under my nose to mask the smell.

"Maybe the turkeys wouldn't have been so bad after all," he grumbled, dabbing antiseptic on his own scrapes as he sat on one of the cots.

"Where's your sense of adventure?"

"I left it behind in Russia that time you decided to blow up an army base."

"You gotta admit, it was a hell of a trip."

He waggled his head from side to side. "Okay, it was."

"And Scotland's pretty. The old house is kinda cool, don't you think?"

"Have you climbed up the tower?"

"Not yet. I think I'd want some kind of safety harness."

"I meant the inside."

"I'm talking about the inside—the roof leaks, and most of the wood in there is rotten."

"Stonework looks okay, though."

"Yeah, it's solid. And it was quite a place a century ago. Aileen from the pub's got a bunch of pictures from the old days." I turned my attention to the skull, sitting in its plastic box on the floor. "Wonder how long our new friend's been here?"

Jane Doe? John Doe? I wasn't an anthropologist, but I suspected the former. The top of the head was rounded rather than blocky, and there was no brow ridge to speak of. This wasn't the first skull I'd seen.

Who had she been?

Where had she lived?

How had she died?

What misfortune had led her to be interred in such a grim resting place?

Sky's voice came from outside. "Uh, you might not want to go in there."

"Why not?"

Shitting hell. Nick jumped up, but it was too late. Fletcher was already inside the stable, his arm wrapped around Paige's waist as if it were surgically attached.

"Ooh, new lights?"

She pointed at the ceiling, and I tried to nudge the skull under a cot with my foot. But the movement drew Fletcher's attention, and of course he knew exactly what he was looking at.

"Is that...?"

Was everyone going to ask the same damn question today?

"There was a small issue with the septic tank."

Paige was still admiring the new strip light Marc had installed. "You found the septic tank?"

"Yeah, we found it."

"What's the issue?"

"There's a body in it."

Well, probably. It was possible our "Beast" had lopped off the head and hidden the rest of the victim elsewhere, but that seemed unlikely. Too labour intensive. Why go to so much trouble when there was a perfectly good disposal site available for the entire thing? Just slide the body in, watch it sink into the murky depths, and drag the cover back over the hatch. Job done.

Paige giggled, blissfully oblivious. "No, tell me really. And what's the weird smell in here? Did another rat die?"

"There really is a body in the septic tank. Well, most of a body."

Now she looked down, and her face morphed into a mask of horror. She got half a scream out before I clapped a hand over her mouth.

"Shhh."

I took my hand away, and she gasped in air. "I'm gonna be sick."

She bolted out of the stable, and when I poked my head outside, Sky was already holding the Portaloo door open. *That's my girl.* Fletcher hurried after Paige as the sound of retching filled the air.

"That went well."

Nick just rolled his eyes as Ross walked in, followed by Marc, AJ, and Griff.

"Someone broke the news to the lass?" Ross asked.

"Yup." I studied each of their faces in turn. "So, what's the verdict?"

I thought I already knew the answer, but I needed to check.

"We're in. Three nights, and if this guy hasn't shown up by Friday, we go to the police."

He'd show up, I was confident of that. I held out a hand.

"Deal."

17

PAIGE

"What if they think it was me? What if the police think I had something to do with it?"

"Relax. They won't."

How could Fletcher stay so calm? *There was a body in my freaking yard!*

"But I own the property."

"And you've only lived there for three months. I may not be a leading expert on human decomposition, but that body's been in the septic tank for longer than that."

Just when I thought this already hellish year in Scotland couldn't get any worse, the devil rolled the dice again. One step forward, two steps back, another step forward...and he pushed me down a flight of stairs.

I realised that in the grand scheme of things, I shouldn't be too upset that the police would have to dismantle the septic tank, but I'd so been looking forward to having actual plumbing, and... Guilt washed over me. *A person was dead.* Fletcher thought it was a woman, an innocent woman, and she'd ended up floating in... Bile rose in my throat again, but there wasn't much left in me to throw up.

Emmy had told me to act normal. Normal! *Just chill and we'll handle it.* The woman was insane.

I'd been pulling my hair out at the roots, quite literally until Fletcher took my hands in his. There was a skull. In my home. A slimy, stinking skull that had once been a person with hopes and dreams for the future. Were her parents looking for her? Did she have brothers? Sisters? Children?

"Here." Fletcher passed me a tissue. "It'll be okay, I swear. Give them a few days."

Emmy had made us leave. Go back to Edinburgh, to the fancy hotel. *Take Paige's mind off things,* she'd said to Fletcher. Come back tomorrow afternoon, keep up the routine. What routine? How could I possibly focus at college? The thought of eating left me nauseated, and I wouldn't be able to sleep. Somehow, we'd ended up in my room on the fourth floor, and I was tempted to walk to the window and jump right out.

"Is this a nightmare? If I wish hard enough, will I wake up?"

"Where do you want to eat tonight? I'll take you anywhere."

"How about Thailand, a week before you left? I really wish I could turn back the clock and kick Jez in the balls."

"You'd have to fight me for that honour." Fletcher tucked a lock of hair behind my ear. "You're wearing the earrings I gave you."

"I never take them out."

He sighed. "I wish we could turn back the clock, too. Do things differently."

"That last night... I almost kissed you," I confessed.

"Yes."

"But you didn't...you know, reciprocate."

"No."

My heart plummeted. Today had been a real roller-coaster ride, and my insides were suffering. Had I misunderstood everything? First, I'd been blind to what a jerk Jez was, and now Fletcher didn't feel the same way about me as I felt about him? But yesterday, he'd said he was keeping me—what had he meant?

His hand moved to the back of my neck. "I'm not the type of guy who steals another man's girl, even if that man is an asshole. Besides, I knew he'd fuck up. It was only a matter of time." Fletcher leaned in close, close enough that his lips brushed my ear. "All I had to do was wait." He feathered soft kisses along my jaw, and I shivered. "But I'll always be sorry that I waited too long."

There was a skull in my home, but suddenly that didn't matter so much because now Fletcher's lips were on mine, gentle but insistent, and I had to wrap my arms around him because my legs would have given way otherwise. Why hadn't I shoved Jez into the Andaman Sea when I had the chance? I could have skipped so much heartache and gotten a taste of Fletcher a whole year sooner.

His tongue teased the seam of my lips, and I yielded, my heart racing. I'd become a passenger in my own life, but at least this part of the journey was pleasurable. Fletcher's hands tangled in my hair as he kissed me breathless. And a part of me, the part that thought a girl like me didn't deserve a man like him, wondered if I was still dreaming.

Finally, we broke apart, and he laid his forehead against mine.

"No more waiting."

"Carpe diem."

"Exactly. Want to order from room service rather than a restaurant?"

"I guess I could try eating something light."

He released me and headed for the desk where the menu awaited, but before he picked it up, he threw me a smouldering glance over his shoulder.

"Good. You'll need the energy later."

Wait, was he suggesting...?

"For what?" I asked, aware that I sounded like a fool but unable to help myself.

"Because unless you tell me to leave, I'm in your bed tonight."

Oh. My. Gosh. And he was just so laid-back about it. So confident. How did I feel about the suggestion? Well, my underwear was melting and I was practically salivating, so there was that.

"Uh, can I see the menu?"

"Sure."

I was going to need at least three courses, plus a gallon of water because staying hydrated was important. Maybe a glass of wine for courage and extra ice cream to cool myself down.

"Do they serve energy drinks?" I asked without thinking.

Fletcher laughed and hooked an arm around my waist. "If they don't, I'll go out and buy you a six-pack."

"No, don't leave!" I clapped a hand over my mouth. "Darn it, now I sound clingy."

"You don't sound clingy."

"I need to learn to think before I speak."

"Your lack of a filter is one of the things I love about you. What you see is what you get. You don't play games."

"If I played games, I'd only get disqualified. I don't understand the rules."

"We can make our own rules." He waved the menu at me. "But after we've ordered dinner."

"What's the budget?"

"Order whatever you want."

"But—"

"I've just spent over a year working in the Antarctic. Got paid good money, and do you know how many retail opportunities there are in the permafrost? I can afford to buy my girl a nice dinner." He ran the tip of his tongue along my ear. "And make no mistake, Paige. You're my girl now."

I swallowed hard. "I'll have the steak."

"Good choice."

"It's lovely to meet you."

Lara opened her arms to hug me, and I liked her instantly. She was so sweet and smiley and warm.

"I'm happy to meet you too."

Despite all the trouble with Glendoon, I'd never missed a college class before. But after Fletcher had once again demonstrated just how sorely Jez had been lacking, I'd barely managed to muster up the energy to send a text to Maria, who sat next to me in our Wednesday-morning Victorian literature seminar, begging her to take notes.

And now I had to survive breakfast with Fletcher's future sister-in-law. That was how he'd described her, although I had to keep quiet because Nick hadn't popped the question yet.

"Isn't this hotel beautiful? And the staff are so nice. Did you get those little chocolates on your pillow?"

Not last night because Fletcher had hooked the *Do Not Disturb* sign over the door handle and then we hadn't left the bed until morning. Were my cheeks red? They sure felt as if they were burning.

"They pay real good attention to detail."

"Nick said you've lived in Scotland for three months?"

"Almost three months." I resisted the urge to add "unfortunately" at the end of the sentence.

"Do you know the good places to visit? Usually, I buy a guidebook before we take a vacation, but this was such a last-minute trip." She giggled. "I even forgot to pack fresh socks."

"Do you need socks? I have extra pairs."

"Oh, the concierge got me some."

Right, because that was how rich people did stuff. "Uh, okay...sightseeing... In Edinburgh itself? There's the castle, the National Gallery, the Palace of Holyroodhouse, the camera obscura..."

"What about that big hill? Can we climb it?"

"Arthur's Seat? It takes around two hours to reach the top, but you can do a shorter walk around the park if you don't have the time."

"Want to come along?"

"I... I..."

Fletcher squeezed my shoulders. His arm had become a permanent fixture around me now.

"Take the day off. You've earned it. Just relax and enjoy yourself, and I'll drive over to Glendoon and see what's going on."

"But I should—"

"There's nothing for you to worry about."

Lara gave my hand a comforting squeeze. "Nick told me about the problems you've been having, and if he says he has it handled, I promise you he does."

That was when it struck me—if things with Fletcher went the way I hoped they did, I wouldn't just gain a boyfriend, I'd end up with a whole new family. Not one related by blood, but a group of people who stuck together and helped each other out when the going got tough. And I really, really liked that idea.

It was getting easier to smile again.

"In that case, I'd love to spend the day with you."

18

EMMY

He didn't show up.

The motherfucker didn't show up.

Had he sensed us out there on the hill? I didn't think so, not unless he was an operator too. More likely, he had family time or work commitments, or he simply overslept, but that still didn't make me any less annoyed after spending the night freezing my ass off.

I'd even started some rumours of my own—told Aileen that we'd heard weird noises in the forest, and Paige had got so scared that she'd gone to stay with a friend in Edinburgh while Sky and I slept in the old stable to prove there was nothing to worry about. Aileen seemed like the type of woman who'd pass gossip on, and there was no harm in giving our suspect false hope that his plan was working. Encouraging him to up his game. But so far, he hadn't taken the bait.

This whole trip had been an exercise in frustration. Not just the Glendoon problem, but the Carmody case too. Hallie's main suspect had been reliant on a wheelchair for six years, so now she had to branch out into other avenues—the mystery kept unravelling, but somehow we never got to the end. She'd managed to collect DNA from Gordon Burns yesterday by cosying up with Dair at the next table when the Burns family went out for a fish supper, then switching Gordon's water glass with her own before the table got bussed at the end of the meal, but now she had to track down Keith Burns and Ronald Burns as well. Forget Thanksgiving—we'd still be here at Christmas.

But I couldn't show my frustration, not when I was the team leader and people were looking at me to, well, lead.

"Good job, guys. We'll do the same again tonight, but Sky, I want to move our position slightly farther up the hill for better visibility. Was everyone else happy?"

A chorus of yeses came.

"Get some rest. I'll pick up breakfast for everyone from the pub, and this afternoon we can do a couple of hours on the wiring since we can't touch the drainage at the moment."

And while I was picking up breakfast, I wanted to get the gossip from Aileen myself. See if anyone from the village had been asking a few too many questions about the goings-on at Glendoon Hall. Our culprit was local, I was certain of that. If he lived out of the area, chances were he wouldn't even have noticed Paige's arrival. She hadn't exactly broadcast her presence.

Plus I needed to see a man about Scotch exports. Although if things carried on as they were, not one damn bottle of single malt would make it to the US. I'd end up drinking the entire output of the distillery myself.

On Thursday morning, a niggle of doubt started to creep in.

We'd spent the night up on the hill again, and the barn owls had been out in full force. Our deer count was in triple figures, and Ross had even spotted a rare polecat, which Fletcher seemed weirdly excited about. Or perhaps it wasn't that weird considering he counted penguins for a hobby. Nick had made the mistake of mentioning the sighting on the phone, and now Fletcher was on his way over with Paige and Lara to "help."

I'd suggested he could help more by staying out of the way, but once he heard about the polecat, that wasn't going to happen.

And now here they were.

Hurrah.

"If you go near the hill, take Nick with you. And don't poke around too much—going about our normal activities is fine, but we don't want to flood the area with people and scare the suspect off."

It was a delicate balance. My chat with Aileen yesterday hadn't yielded any useful leads—apparently Glendoon was a village full of nosy buggers and *everyone* had been asking questions about the big hoose. One or two had enquired whether there might be the possibility of employment if the place was being renovated, and she sensed that Niall-like-the-river Docherty was having regrets over weaselling out of the plumbing job, because his wife was pregnant again and kids weren't cheap, were they?

I'd kept things vague and taken the phone numbers she'd noted down. Said work was progressing as planned and mentioned that the water was running now. Why wouldn't anything shake loose?

"Maybe he's already been spooked off the hill?" Fletcher said. "He was in the trees at the front earlier."

Come again?

"How do you know that?"

"There's a line of fake wolf tracks next to the driveway. I

noticed it when I stopped to look at a nuthatch. Fresh, too. They were definitely made since yesterday's rain."

That conniving bloody sneak.

Fuck.

I should have anticipated that, but even if I had, we didn't have enough manpower to cover all points of the compass. We'd end up with a hole in our net. If I put two people at the front to watch the area near the driveway, that would leave only five of us to cover fifty-plus acres of hillside. Yeah, we could see heat sources from a distance, but we still had to get close enough to identify them and then follow quietly if we struck gold.

We needed more manpower. I'd have to call the London office, or what about Ben Darke? Ben was former military and the brother of a good friend who worked for us occasionally, and he didn't mind bending a few rules. Or...

I felt him before I saw him.

I'd feel him anywhere.

"Surprise, Diamond."

Black. And he had Rafael in tow. All my prayers had been answered.

"What the fuck are you doing here?"

"I couldn't bear to be apart from you for a moment longer."

"Bullshit. You just didn't want to herd turkeys."

"That may have factored into my decision."

"And your sidekick?"

"There was a spare seat on the plane, and it seemed a shame to waste it."

"What plane?" Our long-range jet was already in the UK, and we rarely took the smaller Lear out of the Americas. "Did you fly commercial?"

"Only for the last leg. We hitched a ride to Dublin with James."

On Air Force One. Of course, how could I be so stupid?

"What about the office? Nick's here, and Nate's in Cuba. We shouldn't all be out of the US at the same time."

"Nate's not in Cuba. He's sleeping in the basement at headquarters." Now Black frowned. "Anyone would think you were trying to get rid of me, Diamond."

Shit. "I'm not." The fight went out of me, and I stood on tiptoes to kiss him. "Sorry. I've just had a crappy week, that's all."

"The suspect didn't show up yet?"

"He did, but in the wrong place." I smiled sweetly and lowered my voice. "How do you feel about a little night-time action?"

"The fully clothed kind?"

"Unfortunately, but I'll give you an IOU."

"You always did know how to sweet-talk me." He sighed. "At least this place is turkey-free. One of those fuckers nearly took James's thumb off."

"Ouch."

"He's not Bradley's biggest fan right now."

"How's the round-up going?"

"At last count, Carmen and Slater had darted fifty-seven turkeys and one Canada goose."

"Why the goose? Where did *that* come from?"

"Who knows? But it was limping, so Bradley took it to a veterinarian."

Of course he did. "And where are the turkeys they caught? The ones that didn't get pardoned? Tell me they were on sale or return?"

"The Blackwood Foundation donated enough cash to a wildlife sanctuary to keep the birds for the rest of their natural lives, and the volunteers have been picking them up in batches of ten." Well, that was one kind of solution. Black looked up at the grand old building before us. "So, this is Glendoon Hall?"

"It is. Do you want the tour?"

"Why not? We've got time to kill."

"No, that comes later." Oops. Paige looked a tiny bit horrified at my words. "Chill, I'm joking." I took Black's hand. "Anyhow, come and check out the house. I looked up some stuff about the history—it was built in 1835, but there was another building here before. Apparently, the wine cellar started out as an icehouse, and Aileen from the pub said you can still see the blocked-up drain, but when I poked around down there, all I found was cobwebs and rodents."

"You're really selling this."

"Did I mention there's a ghost?"

"As I said..."

"C'mon, you'll love the stained glass." "Stained" being the operative word. "And what's left of the fancy staircase..."

19

EMMY

This was much better.

I had a good feeling tonight.

There were seven of us on the rear slope, positioned at strategic intervals. I'd put Sky and Rafael at the front, mainly because of her inexperience, but also because I figured a little bonding time wouldn't hurt. Damn, it was cold. I leaned against the remaining wall of the old croft, which was more of a pile of stones by that point, and breathed into my scarf. A plume of steam announcing my presence was the last thing I wanted.

I waited.

And I waited.

Then at five a.m., I felt it. That prickle.

"He's here," I whispered.

Ross was down by the stable block, and tucked in against the rear wall, he had the best view over the whole slope. Half a minute passed before he spoke.

"Coming from the north-east, a third of the way up, I'd say."

Marc and AJ were in the south—eight o'clock and ten

o'clock, if you looked at the slope from the house—and Griff was at the top of the slope beside a well-worn animal track. I'd positioned myself, Black, and Nick to the north—at two, four, and five o'clock—because I figured it was more likely that our man would come from the direction of the village, and I was right. Silently, I began to move downwards to close the distance between us, sticking to the spongy layer of pine needles and leaf litter rather than mud so I didn't leave evidence of my movements.

"Got him on thermal." That was Nick. "He's moving higher."

A howl rolled through the air from our target's direction, low and mournful. Clearly one motion-activated speaker wasn't enough, and he believed in the belt-and-braces approach. Black picked him up next.

"Target's assumed a seated position. Appears to be changing his footwear."

So we'd have another set of paw prints in the morning. For a brief moment earlier, I'd considered knocking together a pair of giant fake lion boots or rigging up yellow LEDs along with some ominous roaring to give him a good scare, but that wouldn't have achieved our goal. Far easier to follow the suspect to his home or vehicle when he wasn't sprinting in terror.

He switched direction and lumbered awkwardly down the hill on a diagonal path, coming within spitting distance of the stable yard. Getting braver? Or merely more desperate?

"Ross, he's in your space."

No answer, but I hadn't expected one. The target was too close. A minute later, he passed within metres of Ross and skirted around the corner of the house. Oh, he'd spent time here. He knew the place well. How many times had he snooped around as Paige slept? Fuck, that didn't bear thinking about.

"Coming your way, Silver," I told Rafael. As a sicario in Colombia, he'd been nicknamed Mercurio, or Quicksilver, and it fit. He seeped through the night like liquid, a molten shadow.

"*Entendido.*"

I'd never liked it, the loss of control. Sitting back and letting others handle the dirty work simply wasn't in my nature. But I trusted Rafael, and I trusted Sky, and at some point, I wanted to retire. Not in the next year and probably not even in the next decade, but someday. And Black was ten years older than me. Just once, I wanted to spend a month or two on the little tropical island he'd bought a few years back, sipping coconut rum and making love on the beach. Carefully. Because sand.

And that meant I needed to practise my delegation skills.

We all made our way carefully down the slope to Paige's stable while Sky and Rafael picked up the trail. The new guard taking over from the old guard. Silence reigned across the airwaves, but that was okay. No news was good news. If there was a problem, we'd be the first to hear about it.

We couldn't risk starting the generator, not with our target still on the move, but we'd filled thermos flasks with coffee earlier, and even though it was more tepid than hot now, the warmth was welcome. I broke out the cookies too. After three freezing nights outside, we deserved them.

Almost twenty minutes passed before Rafael's whisper came over the radio.

"We have an address. On our way back."

I held up my hand for a high five, and Black slapped it. Goal: achieved. Now we could report our finds to the police and our mystery woman could finally be laid to rest.

"Thanks, guys. A job well done."

Ross held up his mug in a toast. "Cheers. Fitting boilers'll be a bit of an anticlimax going forward."

Griff snorted. "At least we won't freeze our arses off overnight."

"True enough. Reckon we can put the generator on now?"

"Reckon we can."

By the time Rafael and Sky slipped inside, the fan heater was working overtime, and Sky parked herself in front of it, rubbing her hands together in an attempt to force some warmth into them.

"Bloody hell. It's colder than a witch's tit out there. I swear it's gonna snow. Is that coffee?"

I passed her a mug. "Decaf."

"Who the hell drinks decaf?"

"I can make you an espresso if you like, but one of us is planning on getting some rest." I tested the temperature of my drink, found it less than scalding, and took a mouthful. "So, decaf?"

"Maybe I'll try it. I mean, it can't possibly taste as gross as that stuff Marisol gave me the other day."

Ah, Marisol. Black's mother, Rafael's grandmother, and a woman who looked so sweet and harmless until you realised she kept a silenced pistol in a custom-made holster under the seat of her wheelchair. You could say assassination was a family business.

"What did she give you?"

Sky screwed up her face, and Rafael filled us in.

"Sabajón."

"Okay, I'm with Sky. That stuff should be banned."

"It's a traditional Colombian recipe."

"That doesn't make it any better." Think eggnog mixed with firewater plus a sprinkling of aniseed in case the concoction wasn't bad enough already. "But can we stick to the subject at hand? Where did our man go?"

"To a cottage called Melrose on Churchview Lane," Sky said. "Any idea who lives there?"

"Not right now, I don't, but sure as hell we'll find out in the morning."

"It's morning now."

"Good luck explaining the story to a detective at this hour."

"Okay, okay. And there're two vehicles on the drive at the cottage—a white transit van and a Honda Civic."

"Did you note down the registrations?"

"Do you think I'm a complete idiot?"

Rafael snorted quietly, and I suppose it *had* been a stupid question.

"We'll follow up tomorrow. I don't suppose our suspect is going anywhere else tonight. He'll need to get some sleep, and we should do the same."

Sky looked doubtfully at the cots. No, nine into four wouldn't go.

"I'll stay here with Black, and I've booked all six rooms at the Glendoon Inn. Two of you will have to share, but there's a rear entrance, so we can come and go as we please. Just keep the noise down because Aileen lives in the attached cottage. Good job tonight, everybody."

"We'll come back early," Ross promised. "This place is gonnae be a circus in the morning."

Yes, yes it was. But as long as I was the ringmaster, I could live with that.

20

EMMY

"The plumber?" Paige's mouth formed an O of shock. "It was the plumber?"

Yes, it was the plumber. Not Ross but Niall fucking Docherty, the "take my advice, hen" plumber who we now knew lived in Melrose Cottage, Churchview Lane. No wonder he hadn't wanted to look for that bloody stopcock.

"But...but I met him. I was here with him alone." She shuddered and curled into Fletcher. "What if he'd tried to kill *me*? No one would ever have found the body."

Probably true, but we didn't yet know his motive. Although we had a good idea of who the victim was. When Dair had run Docherty's name through the computer, he'd found a small article from eleven years ago in the *Stirling News*, a plea for information on a missing girl. She'd gone for an early-morning hike and never returned, and her parents and devastated boyfriend were all desperate for news of her whereabouts.

Devastated boyfriend, my arse. He'd killed her.

He'd killed her and hidden the body.

They'd both lived in Bannockburn at the time—not

together, the article noted—which was perhaps why her disappearance didn't cause much of a stir in Glendoon. A follow-up story mentioned a search-and-rescue team, the possibility of a tragic accident, but now we knew better.

And several years after the event, the man responsible for her death had moved back home to live in his mum's old house.

"Don't dwell on what didn't happen in the past," I told Paige. "If you do that, you'll never be able to enjoy your future."

She glanced towards the house, where a crime scene tent had been set up over the septic tank—good luck with that—and I knew what she was thinking: what future? Hard to move on when her money was tied up in a devil of a restoration project. But with rumours of the Beast put to rest, maybe a buyer would step forward now?

Plus she had Fletcher to lean on. He was already making plans to stick around in Scotland for the rest of the school year. Nick had promised to support them financially until Paige graduated, as long as—and I quote—Fletch didn't sit around on his ass all day. And he wouldn't. He wasn't the type.

"I have a feeling the future will be rosier than you think."

Detective McIntosh poked his head around the door. We'd agreed to stay on site until they'd run out of questions to ask us, and I hoped that time would come soon because the weather hadn't warmed up any. At least I could share Black's body heat. Even sitting on the floor of a dilapidated stable wasn't totally unpleasant as long as he was by my side.

"Mrs. Black, can you spare a few minutes?"

"Sure."

Early this morning, I'd asked Dair to go through his contacts and come up with the name of a decent detective we could call directly. A pragmatic detective. One who wouldn't spend the whole day ball-aching about us using our own initiative to move the case forward. Iain McIntosh had been his answer.

And so far, he seemed competent.

"Could you just walk us through the exact sequence of events that led to you finding the skull? We'll need a statement from you to that effect."

The air outside stank. "Tell me your guys have got Vicks?"

"They've been through a full pot of it already, but there's plenty more in the van."

"What are your plans with the septic tank?"

"Last I heard, they were hoping to remove the top completely. Give themselves more room to work. Do you have any objections to that?"

It wasn't my property, but how much did a new septic tank cost? It wisnae gonnae break the bank, as Ross would say. And I'd seen the pictures of the missing girl, a young brunette with an infectious smile. She deserved peace.

"Do whatever you need to do."

I'd worry about replacing the tank later.

It was ten o'clock in the evening by the time we finally crawled up the stairs at the Glendoon Inn. Black and me, Nick and Lara, Fletcher and Paige, Sky and Rafael, Hallie, Ross, and Marc. AJ and Griff had shared a cab to their respective homes because the fools were meant to be competing in a short-course triathlon in the morning.

Aileen had hovered around all evening, waiting on us hand and foot as well as asking a hundred questions about the police activity at Glendoon Hall. We'd stayed tight-lipped. Okay, we might even have fibbed a bit. Saying we'd found some bones in the old wine cellar was close enough to the truth. The police couldn't arrest Niall Docherty yet, not without a formal identification of the body, and although they were keeping an eye on him, they didn't have the budget for a proper surveillance team. If he felt the heat, I wouldn't have been surprised if he did a runner.

I'd left a bottle of Glendoon Single Malt on the chest of drawers in our room, and I poured us both a nightcap as Black checked his phone.

"What's the turkey count now?"

"Eighty-one down, nineteen to go."

"Hurrah. Maybe we can fly home soon?"

He sat on the bed, back to the headboard and legs stretched out in front of him. "How do you feel about staying in Scotland for a few more days? I've never spent time outside of Edinburgh before."

"Here in Glendoon?"

"Why not?"

"Because you don't fit in the bed properly?"

His feet hung off the end of the mattress unless he lay diagonally, which meant I basically had to sleep on top of him, although I couldn't say I had any complaints about that, so why had I opened my big mouth?

"Are you saying you don't like our sleeping arrangements?"

"I'll ask Aileen if we can extend the booking."

And the answer would be yes. She'd already confessed that this was the first time the inn had been fully booked in over two years, which was a shame because she'd obviously put in an effort to make the rooms comfortable, and whoever was in the kitchen downstairs sure knew how to cook.

Black smiled to himself. "Is this what regular people would call a 'minibreak'?"

"How the hell should I know?"

His smile grew wider, and he held up his glass. "Cheers, Diamond."

I clinked my own glass against it. "Cheers."

He took a sip, and I watched him carefully, hoping that smile wouldn't slip. It didn't.

Phew.

"Not bad. This is made locally?"

"A mile up the road."

"We should pick up a case to take back with us."

"I'm glad you said that because I just bought you the distillery." The paperwork wasn't finalised yet, but I'd shaken on it with Fergus, and he'd proudly informed me that his word was his bond. And besides, we both knew he wasn't going to get a better offer. I crawled up the bed and kissed Black, tasting the Scotch all over again. "I guess that's either a late Happy Thanksgiving or an early Happy Birthday."

Black started laughing, which wasn't quite the reaction I'd expected.

"What's so bloody funny?"

"I suppose we'll be spending more time in Glendoon, then?"

"The place has grown on me, okay? It's peaceful. Well, it is when we're not fishing body parts out of septic tanks. And the scenery's nice to look at."

"I'm glad you said that because I just bought you Glendoon Hall. Happy Thanksgiving-slash-birthday, Diamond."

I spluttered Scotch over him. Shit. What a waste.

"You did what?"

"I saw the way you looked at the place when we were walking around. Don't tell me you didn't think of doing it yourself."

"I did, but how could I justify it? How much time would we be able to spend here?"

"Right now, not much. But there's more to the project than us having an additional vacation home. If Glendoon Hall's restored, the whole village will get a new lease on life."

It would. After the initial restoration, we'd need staff to help look after the place—a caretaker and groundskeepers. And there was nothing to say we needed to use it as a ninth home. Or tenth? Dammit, I'd lost count. We could rent it out, or turn it into a training centre or a wedding venue, or utilise it through the Blackwood Foundation. Securing the future of the distillery would help Glendoon too.

And more than anything, I liked the idea of a quirky old building living to see another century instead of crumbling into the ground. The restoration would be a bitch, but we'd do it right. Glendoon Hall deserved its peace too.

A laugh choked out of me.

"What's so funny?"

"I think we're gonna need to buy a new septic tank."

Then we were both laughing, and then we started pulling each other's clothes off, and yeah, it was a very happy Thanksgiving-slash-birthday indeed.

21

HALLIE

Monday evening, and almost everyone was happy.

Emmy was happy because she owned Glendoon Hall. Paige was happy because she didn't own Glendoon Hall. Black looked uncharacteristically pleased with his new distillery, and apparently the old owner had agreed to stay and manage the place for a few years on a comfortable salary, so he was happy too. Fergus would get to do the parts he enjoyed—making the actual whisky—without having to worry about the bank loans he'd been struggling to repay.

Lara was happy because Nick had finally gotten down on one knee and asked her to marry him. On top of a mountain, no less. Nick was ecstatic because she'd—of course—said yes. They hadn't set a date for the wedding yet, and nobody had dared to break the good news to Bradley. Eloping had been mentioned.

Fletcher was happy because Paige had agreed to move in with him. They absolutely, definitely weren't going to buy another property in Scotland, but there were plenty of comfortable apartments to rent within easy walking distance of the university. Plus a guy Fletcher knew from his time in

Antarctica was running a conservation project in the Scottish Highlands, and would Fletcher be interested in helping out with that?

All the pieces were gradually slotting into place.

Ross, Marc, AJ, and Griff were happy because they'd all be working on the restoration of Glendoon Hall, and that project would keep them busy for months. Maybe even years. The septic tank was empty, and Detective McIntosh was happy because the dental records they had on file for Niall Docherty's missing ex-girlfriend matched the skull, so they had both a known victim and a suspect.

And Sky was happy because Rafael had driven her to Loch Ness yesterday. She hadn't seen the famed monster, but she'd bought little plastic Nessie key rings for everyone. Rafael? Well, he seemed reasonably content, but it was never easy to work out what he was thinking. He wasn't scowling, so I took that as a good sign.

Even Dair was happy because Scotland had won some kind of prize for rugby, which was apparently a Really Big Deal.

What about me? Well, I was the exception, and I was just plain puzzled.

The Blackwood team had gathered for an early dinner in a private dining room at the Caladar Hotel, one last meal together before we scattered to various corners of the world. Nick was going to an industry conference in Italy with Lara tagging along to soak up some culture, Sky and Rafael were heading to South America for a training exercise, and I'd be flying back to Virginia.

As a failure.

"It was meant to be an elimination sample," I said. "We never expected it to match." Three brothers, three DNA samples, and only one had come up trumps. The wrong one. "The evidence says that Gordon Burns left the drop of blood on Mila Carmody's window latch, but there's just no way he could have done it. He was undergoing rehabilitation after a stroke, and he still uses a wheelchair."

"What if he had two strokes?" Sky suggested as she cut into her pizza. She'd ordered it with ham and pineapple, much to Emmy's disgust. "A mild stroke back then, and a more severe one recently?"

"Nuh-uh. The original one left him unable to walk."

Emmy glanced at Black. "He could have a secret twin."

"We checked the birth records, and there was only one baby born. The Burns family seems real stable, and I don't think Mrs. Burns would have given one baby up for adoption and kept the other. She already had a child, and she went on to have two more after Gordon."

"What about death records? Could there have been a stillborn child that wasn't really stillborn? There've been cases in the past—mothers being told a child died when an unscrupulous doctor gave it to another couple for adoption in return for a nice fat backhander."

Rafael took a sip of his beer. I'd never seen him drink beer before, not once, but tonight he'd decided to celebrate along with everyone else.

"What if there's a simpler explanation?" he asked. "Contamination in the Carmody sample?"

"That's possible, but we still can't explain how Gordon Burns's DNA got from Scotland to a lab in the US."

"There was a case in Europe where the police thought they had a serial killer on the loose based on DNA results, and the DNA turned out to belong to a woman at the factory that made the swabs. What does Burns do for a living?"

"He worked in the customer service department of a bank for the ten years before his stroke."

Dair spoke up. "And before that, he was an insurance advisor."

"Did he ever donate blood for medical purposes?" Black asked. "Can we find that out?"

"One step ahead of you there." I managed a smile. Gordon Burns had even been featured in the *Midlothian Advertiser* after his hundredth donation. "Yes, he is a donor, but what are the odds of someone stealing his blood and flying it all the way to Virginia to leave at a crime scene? Plus he had the stroke six months before Mila disappeared—wouldn't he have been too focused on his own health at that time to keep donating?"

"Want me to quote Sherlock Holmes?" Nick asked. "'When you've eliminated the impossible, whatever remains, however improbable, must be the truth.' Maybe someone froze the blood?"

A blood popsicle? Ick.

"There is one other option."

Everyone turned to look at Fletcher.

"Have you heard of a chimera?" he asked.

Sky stuck up her hand. "I know this one. It's a beast with the body of a lion, the tail of a serpent, and an extra goat head stuck on for shits and giggles."

"No, that's *the* Chimera. I'm talking about *a* chimera."

"What's the difference?"

"A chimera is, at its simplest, one organism that contains two sets of DNA. When I was at Princeton, I roomed with a biochemist who was doing research into Parkinson's disease, and he worked with mouse-human chimeras."

"So...what are you saying? Now we're looking for a mutant mouse?"

"No, that was just an example. We also had several conversations about human chimeras. Mr. Burns donated blood, but did he ever donate bone marrow?"

"Why?"

"Because in a bone marrow transplant, the recipient's own bone marrow is destroyed and replaced with marrow from the donor. That marrow contains stem cells, those stem cells make blood cells, and those blood cells will be genetically identical to the donor, not the recipient. In cases where all of a person's bone marrow is replaced, you get a human chimera. Their blood has one genetic profile, and the rest of the cells in their body have another. So, did Mr. Burns donate?"

That was a question I couldn't answer. "I don't know, but he seems like the altruistic kind."

How could we find out for sure? Interviewing him would be awkward because how could we explain tracking him down in the first place? He'd feel we'd invaded his privacy, which we had, so that was understandable, but it left us with a problem.

"Isn't there a global bone marrow register?" Emmy asked. "That might explain how Burns's DNA ended up in the US."

Black just picked up his phone. "Anyone got a phone number for Burns?"

"Uh, yes?"

"Good." He put a finger to his lips. "Shhh."

Two minutes later, he was on the phone to Gordon Burns.

"This is Charlie Green from the NHS Blood and Transplant team." To my ears, Black's English accent sounded flawless. "We're carrying out a study on the long-term health of bone marrow donors, and I'm hoping you have two minutes to answer a few simple questions." A pause. "Can I first confirm that you've donated bone marrow in the past? ... Thank you, yes." A longer pause, one that stretched interminably. "A stroke? I'm sorry to hear that. ... No, no, I'm not aware of any connection, but I'll pass that information on to the researchers. I hope you have a good week, sir."

"Well?" I leaned forward in my seat, my dinner cold now. Who cared about food? "Did he?"

"Eleven years ago."

"Who to?"

Sky held up her phone. "The website says they protect the

privacy of donors and recipients. You don't find out who gets your gloop."

"Then we're at a dead end? We can't ever solve the Carmody case?"

Somewhere in the United States, a sick-minded transplant recipient was walking free, and there wasn't a damn thing we could do about it?

Black took a sip of wine. "We should hand the next part of the investigation over to the cyber team. The answer we need is hidden in a database, and we're not going to find it in rural Scotland. Put the case on the back burner, top up your glass, and let's enjoy the remainder of our time here."

"It feels like we're giving up."

"We're not giving up. We're proceeding in the most appropriate manner under the circumstances. You've done a good job. *Both* of you have done a good job." He nodded toward Dair. "But you can't let this take over your life."

Mila Carmody's face haunted me at night, a little girl I'd never met, never would meet, but whom I felt I'd come to know. No, I wouldn't give up. I'd never give up.

But Black was right. There were other cases, other victims, and I couldn't neglect them.

I couldn't neglect Ford either. Or my friends, or my parrot.

And who the heck was Mike?

22

HALLIE

N *early two months later...*

There was frost on the ground when I landed in Oregon on a crisp January morning.

After the Thanksgiving turkey debacle, Christmas had been a comparatively subdued affair with only eleven Christmas trees at Riverley—I'd counted—and a minor incident when the power to the ice-skating rink failed and we ended up with a very shallow swimming pool instead.

Plus Emmy had found the time to hunt stolen antiquities in Egypt, but that was a whole other story. Sometimes, I thought she was a cyborg. She never stopped. Throughout December, the cyber team had also been working overtime, including tiptoeing their way carefully through the security loopholes of various hospitals and other related organisations while chomping on sugar cookies and nibbling mince pies.

And they'd found us a name.

Jonathan Snyder.

Thirty-three years old, Yale-educated, a nondescript brown-haired man who managed to look slightly nervous in every photograph I'd seen of him. Was there a reason for that? After completing a PhD in history—pre–Civil War American history, to be precise—he'd worked as a teacher for a year and then quit unexpectedly, much to the disappointment of his students. The three I'd spoken with had sung his praises. He planned to move out of state, he'd told his former boss in Connecticut, but the man had never received a request for a reference. Never heard from Jonathan Snyder again.

He'd just...vanished.

His social media profiles went dead, and when I'd gotten in touch with his friends, they'd all told me the same story— Snyder said he was moving to take up a new role, but he'd never actually said what that role was. His mom was still alive, welcoming when I visited, and she thought he was holed up somewhere quiet, writing a book. He liked to write. She received letters from him regularly, and didn't he have neat handwriting? I'd been more interested in the envelopes. They'd all been postmarked from Coos Bay, Oregon, population seventeen thousand.

I'd scanned a couple of the letters, and they were the kind of waffle that went on and on without saying anything. The book was coming along nicely, he'd been for several long hikes, he'd gotten a flat tyre on the highway the other day but thank goodness Pop had taught him to always carry a spare. His mom was sweet, and I felt guilty for lying to her, for spinning a story about being an old friend from Jonathan's Yale days when really I was looking to send him to jail.

A little more digging revealed that a Jonny Snyder had been crowned employee of the month last March at a sporting goods store in North Bend, Oregon, and the small write-up on their blog included a photo.

It was the same guy.

We were closer than we'd ever been before, but were we close enough?

Soon, we'd find out.

Now we were on our way to speak with him, and when I said "we," I meant me, Emmy, and Ana. The two of them had travelled to California several days ago on another job, but that was wrapped up now—the fact that Ana was involved made me think that the "wrapped up" part might be literal because she probably got a bulk discount on body bags—and when I'd called Emmy to update her on developments, she'd volunteered to fly up and help me. Ana had offered her services too, which made me slightly nervous, especially after the way girls' night had turned into World War III last month, but we all wanted to see the case closed.

To see justice.

Speaking of closed cases, Niall Docherty had finally been arrested, and when confronted with the evidence—the body, our statements on his antics at Glendoon Hall, and the concrete "wolf" shoes the police had found in his shed—he'd confessed to hiding his ex-girlfriend's body. He claimed her death was an accident, that they'd had a fight and she'd hit her head when she tripped over, but the knife marks the medical examiner had found on her ribs told a different story. A jury would have to decide which story they believed, but either way, he'd be going to prison.

In a happier ending, Paige and Fletcher had moved into an apartment two minutes from the university, and Paige had sent the sweetest thank-you notes to everyone involved. She had her life back, she said, and her relief came through in her words. Now she spent her days studying Shakespeare and Kafka while Fletcher monitored red squirrels in the Highlands.

I checked my watch. Emmy and Ana were due to land in fifty minutes, and then we had a four-hour drive from

Portland to North Bend. Blackwood's Portland office had delivered a pool vehicle to the airport, and Bradley had arranged our accommodation, so even if this trip was a bust, at least I'd get a good night's sleep. Bradley *always* went for five stars. He was in Oregon too, visiting a friend in Eugene.

I grabbed a coffee and a magazine, then took the weight off my feet while I waited for Emmy and Ana's plane. And it really was Emmy's plane. She had a private jet. There were perks to marrying a billionaire, but I'd still never trade Ford for a man like Black. Ford was *everything*. He'd moved into my and Mercy's apartment when I returned from Scotland, and the week before Christmas, we'd sailed his yacht to its new slip in Virginia Beach. Now we'd be able to spend weekends on the water and actually go somewhere. I couldn't wait. This time last year, I'd been a prisoner, and now I had my whole life to look forward to.

One more coffee later, the two musketeers strolled into the arrivals hall, duffel bags in hand.

"Ready to go?" Emmy asked.

"Definitely."

Maybe we'd make it to North Bend before Jackson's Sporting Goods closed for the day? When Emmy climbed into the driver's seat of the black SUV, I crossed myself, and I wasn't even Catholic. It just seemed like a smart idea with her behind the wheel.

"That's him?" Emmy asked.

"I think so." I checked the picture on my phone again. "Yup."

"Then let's go."

We'd arrived outside the sporting goods store with an hour

to spare, although the stress of the journey had taken at least a year off my life. If there was a dubious call to be made at a stoplight, then Emmy made it. Ana seemed remarkably unruffled, further reinforcing my suspicion that she wasn't even human.

The fast-food joint opposite had windows that faced the Jackson's parking lot, and we'd settled in to wait with milkshakes, burgers, and fries, plus extra onion rings and a slice of apple pie for Emmy. Where did she put it all? She was just finishing the last mouthful when our target appeared.

I followed her and Ana out to the car, wishing I'd remembered to pee when I had the opportunity. *Please, don't let Jonathan Snyder live too far away.*

He climbed into a red SUV and trundled off, heading south, sticking to the speed limit or staying just below. Careful, but not overly cautious. And whose name was the car registered in? It wasn't his—I'd checked.

Emmy tutted, annoyed at being forced to drive sedately for once. The scenery in these parts was pretty—hills and forests, glimpses of the sea to the west—but not as starkly beautiful as the Scottish Highlands. Would I ever go back there? I hoped to take Ford one day. Emmy said that when Glendoon Hall was back to its best, any of us were welcome to visit.

Sometimes, I had to pinch myself over the life I led now.

Welcome to Baldwin's Shore. The sign flashed by on the right, and I breathed a sigh of relief. Our hotel was also in Baldwin's Shore—the best in the area, Bradley assured us—and if Snyder lived close by, I'd be able to use the bathroom soon.

As if by magic, Snyder put on his turn signal and swung right into a residential street. Emmy hung back for a moment, then followed.

"There it is," Ana murmured.

The red SUV was parked outside a small ranch house. A

white picket fence bordered a tidy lawn, and as we drove past, a small girl ran out of the front door and threw herself into his arms. He had a daughter? None of the people I'd spoken to had mentioned that or even hinted at it. A woman stood in the lit doorway, and her gaze followed our vehicle. Emmy didn't stop, just kept rolling slowly as if we were looking for the right address. Thankfully, the road curved out of sight a hundred yards ahead, so we didn't have to keep up the pretence for long.

And when she pulled over around the bend, she leaned her head against the steering wheel and let out a long groan.

"I don't bloody believe it."

"Believe what? That he has a family? I know it's weird, but—"

"Not that. Didn't you recognise the woman at the door?"

"No?"

"It's been a while since I saw her, but five bucks says that was Cassandra Traynor."

Cassandra Traynor? The name was familiar, and I quickly sifted through the reams of information in my head. *Cassandra Melanie Traynor.*

"Mila's older sister?"

"Half-sister. Same mom, different dad. Fuck me, we always said it was an inside job, but we were looking at the wrong insider."

"But why would she...?"

"I don't know. How old do you think that kid with her is?"

"Uh, eleven or twelve?" A jolt of realisation shot through me as I understood what Emmy was saying. "You think that was *Mila Carmody*?"

I'd always assumed she was dead. We all had. So long had passed, and the statistics said... *Screw statistics.* There was a chance Mila was alive.

"I should tell Ford," I muttered.

"No," Emmy snapped, and I recoiled on instinct. "You absolutely shouldn't tell Ford. If Cassandra Traynor took Mila, I'm betting there was a damn good reason, and we need to find out what it was before we get the police involved."

"But—"

"I was afraid of this. Hallie, there are going to be times when your relationship with Ford clashes with your job. His world is black and white. He took an oath, has rules to follow. We're more...grey."

"You're saying I should keep this from him?"

"I'm saying you should wait for more facts before you set something in motion that you might later regret."

It didn't sit right with me. None of this sat right with me, and I was still trying to process the fact that Cassandra might have kidnapped her own sister. I trusted Ford. But I also trusted Emmy. And I knew from my own experiences in Florida that when in possession of information, law enforcement wouldn't necessarily do the right thing. Ford would, but some of his colleagues were real assholes.

"How will we get more facts?"

"Easy. Tomorrow morning when the kid's at school and Jonathan Snyder's gone to work, we'll have a nice little chat with Cassandra Traynor."

23

HALLIE

"Hi, Cassandra."

Emmy kept her tone light and wore a smile, but Cassandra still tried to slam the door on us. Ana was waiting at the rear of the house in case she tried to make a run for it, but Emmy kicked the door so it bounced back and hit Cassandra in the face. A second later, blood began dripping from her nose.

"Ah, shit," Emmy muttered.

I found a package of tissues in my purse and held it out, but Cassandra was already backing away. We'd waited for hours to speak to her. After the school run, she'd gone to some kind of painting class at a craft store—Bradley would have been in heaven there—and then she'd stopped at a café for coffee, and then she'd bought groceries. The busy life of a child abductor.

"What do you want from me?"

Emmy followed her inside. "Just the truth. Why did you do it?"

Cassandra made a visible attempt to pull herself together.

154

"I don't know what you're talking about. Get the hell out of my house before I call the sheriff."

"Go right ahead. And when he gets here, we'll show him a picture of Mila Carmody and ask him if he sees the similarity between her and your 'daughter.'"

"I... I..."

"Sit down."

Cassandra sank into an armchair in the living room, and now tears streaked her cheeks, mingling with the blood. I offered the tissues again, and this time she took them. Her hands were shaking.

Emmy took a seat opposite and leaned back, legs crossed at the ankles. To an outsider, she might have looked relaxed, but I knew she was anything but.

"We've met before, Cassandra. Do you remember?"

She gave the tiniest shake of her head.

"Four and a half years ago at your mom and stepdad's place. They hired us to find Mila, and we asked to speak with all of her family members. Gotta give you credit, honey. You had us fooled with your 'I wasn't even here but please find my baby sister' act."

Cassandra's features hardened. "You're one of the private investigators."

"That's right."

"Well, you weren't very good. Mom said you thought Uncle Colin took Mila."

Emmy shrugged off the insult. "We're here now, aren't we?"

Cassandra flinched. "But Derrick fired you."

Derrick was her stepfather.

"Yeah, I know, but sometimes we get curious and keep nosing around on our own. It's a bad habit. So, why'd you do it?"

Silence.

"This isn't going away, Cassandra. If you won't talk to us, you can talk to the cops. To be honest, I'm not really fussed which option you pick. Our part's over now. Mila can go home, and when you're behind bars, you'll have all the time in the world to reflect on what you did."

"No!" Cassandra leapt to her feet, but Emmy didn't move. "You can't send her back to him. *You can't.*"

"To who, Cassandra? To Derrick?"

She choked out a strangled laugh. "To our *grandfather.*"

A chill ran through me as I frantically tried to put the pieces together. Emmy, as usual, was ten steps ahead.

"You're saying your grandfather abused her?"

"Abused *us.*" Cassandra's voice rose, bordering on hysterical. "That sadistic son of a bitch abused *us.*"

She sank back into the chair, and then seemed to collapse in on herself with her knees drawn up to her chin and her arms wrapped around her legs. Apart from her sobs, the house was silent. I thought back to the file. Emmy hadn't been a million miles away from solving the case, even back then. She'd gotten bad vibes from the grandfather, focused in on him straight away, but his alibi had checked out. Then the focus had shifted to Mila's uncle. That had made her father unhappy, because who wanted to believe their brother was a suspect? So he'd done the logical thing and kicked us off the case.

Emmy didn't seem inclined to move, and I couldn't just leave Cassandra on her own to fall apart, so I crouched beside her and laid a hand on her arm.

"I'm so sorry you had to go through that."

"Years, it went on for *years.* Grandfather got his hands on Mila once, only once, and I swore to her that it would never happen again. Put me in jail if you must, but don't send her back to that...that m-m-monster."

If I'd learned one thing throughout this long and winding case, it was that monsters came in all shapes and sizes, but a lot of the time, they looked like regular people. Sometimes, they even wore expensive suits and had powerful friends in high places. I'd studied the Carmody file. Cassandra's grandfather was wealthy—not Emmy-and-Black wealthy, but still more than comfortable—and he counted politicians and Wall Street titans among his friends. But under the veneer, it seemed the devil's blood ran through his veins.

"Start at the beginning," Emmy said. "Tell us what happened."

"Aren't you going to read me my rights?"

"We're not the police. None of this is admissible in court. And at the end of the day, we're going to do what's best for Mila. Do you want something to drink?"

Cassandra shook her head. "I feel s-s-sick. I always knew this would catch up with us, but I hoped... I guess I just hoped we'd have more time. Sophie's twelve now..." A faint smile touched Cassandra's lips. "Sophie. We call her Sophie—it's her middle name. The nightmares are almost gone, and she's doing so well in school. She has friends, and a cat, and she's learning to play the flute..."

"Not the violin?" Emmy asked.

I recalled that Cassandra had been a violinist. She'd attended Yale too, on a music scholarship, and she'd been destined for great things until her career just...fizzled out. Now we knew why that had happened.

"Never the violin. With her musical ear, she'd probably be too good at it, and we can't draw attention to ourselves here."

"Okay, from the top. Don't leave anything out."

"We..." Cassandra sucked in a ragged breath. "I was eight years old. Eight years old when Grandfather started with me. We were staying at his home—we often did—and he came in the middle of the night. Told me it would be our little secret, that I was such a good girl and that in time, it would stop hurting and I'd enjoy it. *Enjoy it*," she spat. "He was raping me."

"Did you tell anybody?"

"He told me that if I did, my mom would be angry, and I wouldn't want to upset her, would I? One time, I cried out, and he slapped me." Cassandra flinched. "I can still feel the sting of his hand. So it carried on, and on, and on. I tried to run away, but the police found me and brought me home again. Mom told them I was troubled and promised to take me to a therapist, but she never did. *Troubled*."

"What about your father?"

"He wasn't around much. Some big-shot lawyer who spent most of his time in the courtroom. They married young, you know. Mom was only eighteen when she had me, and I think it was an accident. And then he died when I was fourteen. Until then, the abuse had been... Bearable's the wrong word. But it only happened when we stayed at Grandfather's house, so once or twice a month, and I guess I learned to block it out. Then suddenly, Dad was gone, and we were moving in with Grandfather. I couldn't... I just couldn't deal with it. That was when I told Mom what he was doing."

"She didn't stop it?"

"No! She said..." Cassandra swallowed hard, and I checked around for a trash can in case she got the urge to vomit. She looked kind of green. "Mom said that it was his way of showing us that he loved us." She gave a hollow laugh, but there was no mirth in it. "When I turned eighteen, I got my DNA tested to make sure my grandfather wasn't also my father." A sigh. "But you said to go from the top, and now I'm jumping ahead."

I couldn't see a trash can, but I did spot a row of pictures on the mantel shelf. Cassandra and Jonathan with Mila on the beach, at the park, in a restaurant. Mila wore her hair with bangs now, and it was amazing how much it changed her face, but she seemed happy. In every photo, she was smiling. They all seemed happy.

Cassandra continued, "I cut my wrists, but Mom took me to the hospital, and I remember the doctor asking me so many questions, like why had I done it and was I getting bullied and why was I crying? And the whole time, Grandfather was standing on the other side of the curtain and I couldn't say a word."

"The doctor could have called the police."

"Oh, please. Grandfather was a good friend of Chief Garland. How far do you think my complaint would have gone?"

Considering Chief Garland had been outed as a paedophile himself last year, not very far. That Christopher Pender—Cassandra's grandfather—was another pea from the same pod shouldn't have come as a great surprise. Emmy appeared to agree with that assessment.

"Fair enough. So you kept your mouth shut?"

"I stayed quiet like a good little girl, and now I always have to wear long sleeves. But I survived. I survived his abuse for two more years, and every night I'd lie there wondering if I should swallow all the sleeping pills from the bottle I'd hidden. Mom popped those pills like candy, and every so often, I'd steal one. She never noticed. I had over a hundred in the end."

"But you didn't."

"No, I didn't."

"What changed?"

"*I* changed. I learned, and I grew. I'm as tall as my grandfather now, did you know that? Plus I was heavier back then. I used to comfort eat, and Grandfather hated it, which was why I ate even more. But I ended up with a weight advantage. And I knew he'd never stop. Mom had made her choice in staying, and I had to make mine. So I got a knife."

Oh, this was getting dark.

"You tried to kill him?" I blurted.

"Kill him? I didn't want to go to jail. Why trade one prison for another? No, I pinned him to the bed, put the knife to his throat, and told him that he was done touching me. *Done*. That I'd finished being his victim, and if he didn't send me to boarding school the very next day, I'd wait until he was asleep and then I'd cut his fucking dick off." Finally, Cassandra managed a smile. "I went to boarding school. And I also learned that underneath all his bluster and his threats, my grandfather was a coward."

Emmy nodded. "Men like that always are. The bigger the talk, the smaller the balls. How was boarding school? Where did you go?"

"I attended Shadow Falls Academy, and I loved it. The staff were wonderful, and I made so many new friends... I'd fallen behind at school, but the tutors helped me to catch up enough to get into Yale, and I swore I'd never go home again. It was such a shame what happened to the school. Did you hear? One of the principals died in a terrible car accident last year, and then there were so many awful accusations made... I only hope that other girls get the same chances as I did to learn there."

Good thing Sky hadn't come along for the ride with us because she'd had a hand in helping that teacher off the road. But Cassandra's choice of school figured—Shadow Falls had placed top in every league for arts-based education.

"I'm sure the school will live up to its reputation again," Emmy said. "But you did go home, didn't you? When I spoke with your mom, she said you'd had a rocky relationship in the past, but you were repairing it."

"We weren't repairing anything. I just got better at lying." Another sigh. "I thought I was done with that den of incest for good, but Mom got married again. I couldn't freaking believe it! Did you know Derrick was her personal trainer?

He was only in it for the money, that much I know for certain."

"Did he get along with your grandfather?"

"He had to. Where do you think the money comes from? At heart, Derrick's not an awful person, but he's greedy and he's immature. He's only two years older than me, for goodness' sake. And then Mom ended up pregnant, and I got sucked into the nightmare all over again because I feared that as long as my grandfather was still breathing, he'd go after Sophie."

"That was when you began working your way back into your mother's life?"

Cassandra nodded. "I started visiting her. Not my grandfather, *never* my grandfather, but I needed to get to know my sister. To make her trust me enough to tell me if he came. *When* he came. I guess there was some stupid part of me that thought maybe he wouldn't, that he'd changed after I threatened him, but of course he hadn't. She was seven years old, a year younger than me, and I'll always regret waiting. But I needed to prepare. *We* needed to prepare."

"When you say 'we,' you're talking about Jonathan?"

"Jonny, yes." Another sob. "He's been my rock through all this, even when he was sick, and... That part doesn't matter." Except it did. It was the whole reason we were here. "We met at Yale, and love was the last thing I was looking for, but I found it anyway. I tried to leave him, you know. I told him what I planned to do, that I intended to take Sophie as far away from Grandfather as possible and live off-grid, but he said he'd be damned if he was going to let me do that alone. So we took her together, and then we came here. Mom thinks I'm working as a violin teacher in Connecticut."

"You still visit her?"

"A couple of times a year. Have to keep up the pretence while I wait for Grandfather to breathe his last, don't I?

Although knowing my luck, he'll live to be a hundred. Anyhow, I go during the school breaks. We pretend we're taking family vacations—Jonny and Sophie go to visit with his parents, and I fly to Virginia to do my duty."

"His parents are in on this?"

"No, oh, no. They think I got legal guardianship of my little sister after our parents died in a car accident." Cassandra threw her hands in the air. "It's just one big tower of lies, and I suppose I was always waiting for it to come crashing down. What's going to happen now? Will I go straight to jail?" She put her head in her hands. "Colt's gonna have to arrest me, isn't he? What will I tell him?"

"Who's Colt?"

"The sheriff's deputy on duty today. He lives next door. I've been minding his little girl after school for the past five years. Honestly, I thought the game was up months ago—he got a new girlfriend, and she has a security team, and I know darn well they background-checked me." Now that Cassandra had started talking, it was as if she couldn't stop. Perhaps she was relieved to finally get this off her chest? Bottling everything up for most of her life couldn't have been easy or healthy. "But I guess since I've known Colt for so long, they must've done the lite version because I'm still here. And it's not as if I have a criminal record, not yet. Hell, I've never even gotten a speeding ticket."

"Impressive. I get one of those most months."

"Then maybe you should drive slower?"

"It's an option, yes."

Cassandra straightened. "I'm not going down without a fight. I'm going to tell the world what Grandfather did. When I turned thirty, I got access to my trust fund, and I've saved every single cent of it to pay for legal representation. He can't get his hands on Sophie again. It's simply not an option. And my mom, she's not fit to parent a rock. I hope Derrick leaves her." Then she slumped. "So, what happens now? Sophie will be home from school soon. Brie's picking her up today, but...but...when she gets here, she's going to know there's something wrong."

Emmy just smiled. "I'll defer to Hallie on that question."

She waved a hand in my direction, and my eyes bugged out. What the heck?

24

HALLIE

"U h..."

Emmy's face remained impassive. "We always said this job would come with difficult decisions."

It took a moment to understand what she was asking of me. And when I did, I wanted to curse her out, but I couldn't, not in front of Cassandra. I'd always known that Emmy and the others she worked with dispensed a special brand of justice based on their own moral code, and that code didn't always align with the law as it was written. They weighed up a situation, analysed the pros and cons of any course of action, and then made their choice.

Now she was asking me to do the same.

Should we hand this over to the police and bring the full weight of the law down on Cassandra Traynor and Jonathan Snyder? Or should we walk away?

I scrubbed my hands across my face. How could she ask me to make this choice? I was only twenty-four, barely starting to live my own life. But Emmy had been pushed to act as judge and jury when she was younger than me, hadn't she? At eighteen, she'd been working for Blackwood, and at twenty, she'd been a full-fledged assassin.

Okay, okay... The logical option, the legal option, would be to call Ford. To tell him what we'd found and let him set the wheels of justice in motion. But would it really be justice? I looked across at the photos on the mantel again. *A happy family.* One call, and I'd rip their lives apart. A twelve-year-old girl would be dragged back to Virginia, at best into the care of a money-grubbing, freshly divorced father, at worst into the arms of a grandfather who'd sexually abused her.

Mila Carmody was the girl I'd promised to help. But how would I be helping her if I sent the people who loved her, the people who cared for her, to prison?

"I..." The words stuck in my throat, and I swallowed hard. "I have a question."

Cassandra just stared at me.

"That night, the night Mila was taken. Who opened the window?"

"She did. She knew Jonny and I were coming. I wanted to go by myself, but he said that if anyone was going to get caught, it should be him. That if we were spotted, I should take Sophie and run." Another tear rolled down her cheek. "He's only ever tried to protect both of us. We'd gotten married the week before, and..." A sob burst from her throat. "We were meant to be on our honeymoon."

They'd both given up everything for Mila—Jonathan had quit his teaching job, and Cassandra had turned her back on a musical career. They'd *both* protected her.

"Why Baldwin's Shore?"

"It's far, far away from Virginia. People are always coming and going, so it's easy to stay under the radar, and most of the people here are real nice."

"How did she know you and Jonny were coming?"

"I gave her a phone. A really small one with the buttons. She kept it hidden in Biggles the bunny—that was her favourite toy—and the charger was in her dollhouse." Well, that was a detail the police had missed. "At night, we'd call each other. Mom paid about as much attention to Sophie as she did to me, so she never realised how often we spoke."

Mila had wanted to leave.

She'd made her choice, and now I had to make mine.

But choosing to do the right thing would mean lying to Ford, or at least not telling him the whole truth. If Emmy were in my shoes, would she tell Black everything? Probably. But they were so perfectly matched, and if I stood back and looked at the situation objectively, Ford and I had fundamental differences. He believed in upholding the law, while I'd had enough bad experiences with the authorities to foster a healthy distrust of men who carried the badge.

Hell, how had we even fallen in love?

Because the heart did its own thing.

And for the only case we'd worked together, we'd started off on opposing sides before meeting—more or less—in the middle. Ford had bent the rules he was so fond of, and I'd learned to see the world from more than one perspective. I thought of other couples I knew that somehow made it against the odds—Ana and Quinn, a Russian spy dating a CIA agent. Georgia and Xav, a senator's daughter and—I suspected—a hitman. Dan and Ethan, an all-around badass and a chilled-out music producer. Opposites really did attract.

If we walked away from the Snyders, what on earth would I tell Ford? I thought back a couple of months, to Rafael's comments at that final dinner in Scotland... Police in Europe once thought they had a female serial killer on the loose, when in fact there was contamination from the swab factory. Could I do something with that?

"Has Jonny ever worked in a factory? Somewhere that manufactures windows? Or a warehouse that stores them?"

The slightest smile played across Emmy's lips, while Cassandra just looked plain puzzled.

"No, nothing like that."

"Has he ever made deliveries? Driven a truck?"

"He worked on the docks in Coos Bay for a while, unloading cargo and stacking it onto trucks. And I guess there might have been windows? But I don't understand—what does that have to do with anything?"

"When Jonny went to pick up Mila, he cut himself on the window latch. There was a tiny drop of blood. That's how we found you. But if there was another explanation for the blood being there, then *maybe* this avenue of investigation could wind up as a dead end."

"I..." Understanding dawned. "I see. Well, I'm certain there were *definitely* windows on those trucks."

"We'll want to meet Sophie. See for ourselves that she's happy here."

"Okay, okay, sure. She'll be home in..." Now Cassandra was falling over herself to be helpful, and she checked her watch. "Twenty minutes? Or a little longer if Brie detours by Aaron and Romi's place? Those are friends of ours, and they picked up a new puppy from the shelter this week. Sophie's been so excited to meet it."

"We can wait."

We'd waited for years already. What difference would another half hour make?

In the end, we stayed for dinner. Only Emmy and me—Ana didn't do well in social situations, Emmy said, so she'd headed back to the hotel. Jonny was understandably nervous to see us there, but once Cassandra—now Meli—had taken him aside and explained what was happening, he warmed up.

Sophie chattered away while Meli was cooking and

insisted on playing the flute for us, just an ordinary little girl. And if there was ever any doubt that we were doing the right thing, it was erased when Emmy casually mentioned over dessert that she knew Grandfather Pender. The effect was instantaneous. Sophie froze, and all the colour drained out of her face.

"No," she whispered, then looked to Cassandra for help.

"You don't need to go back, sweetie. Nobody will make you go back."

"Do you promise?"

"I promise."

"We all promise," I added.

Sophie Snyder was staying in Baldwin's Shore where she belonged. And judging by the pensive look on Emmy's face, it wouldn't surprise me if Christopher Pender didn't live to see his hundredth birthday or even his next one.

That night, I had an awkward video conversation with Ford. He didn't realise it was awkward, of course, but the words scratched at my throat as I forced them out with what I hoped was a "you win some, you lose some" expression.

"It was a wasted journey, but the town's pretty. Right by the sea. Bradley found us an amazing hotel, and I can see the beach from my room."

"Jonathan Snyder wasn't the right guy?"

"The blood was his—he definitely had a bone marrow transplant eleven years ago—but he was on his honeymoon when Mila was snatched. His wife confirmed it, and they even showed us their wedding album."

"Where was the honeymoon?"

"They rented a car and made a road trip across the US.

There's no way he could've stashed Mila in the car without his wife noticing."

Which of course Meli had. They'd had clothes ready for Sophie, and Meli had cut her hair with scissors in the morning. Sophie had ridden from Virginia to Baldwin's Shore in the back seat of an old Cadillac, hiding in plain sight as they stopped at various attractions on the way. The freedom ride, Sophie called it.

"Then how did his blood get onto Mila's window?"

"Jonathan takes side jobs while he's writing his book, and one of those jobs involved loading and unloading cargo. Do you know when the windows in the Carmody home were installed?"

Because I did—barely a year before Mila was taken. Blackwood's file on her disappearance had been comprehensive, and it wasn't beyond the realm of possibility that the tiny speck of blood had stuck around for that long.

"I'll look into that. Does this mean you're coming home?"

"We're planning to fly back tomorrow evening. Since we have the jet here, we need to wait for Alex to finish running a half-marathon in Portland so he can hitch a ride with us. And Bradley's over in Eugene, so he's coming too."

"Do I know Alex?"

"He's Emmy's personal trainer."

"The big Russian guy? He doesn't look like much of a runner."

I couldn't help giggling, both with relief that Ford wasn't asking more questions and at the thought of Alex running.

"He lost a bet with Emmy, and the half-marathon is his punishment."

"Remind me never to make a bet with Emmy."

"You and me both. How was your day? Did Detective Duncan get busted down to traffic yet?"

"I live in hope. My day was okay, mostly paperwork, but

enough talk about work. There are much, much better ways of spending an evening on the phone with you."

My insides puddled. Phone sex might have been a new thing for me, but Ford had proven himself to be the master.

"I love you."

"I love you too. Now take off your shirt, plum."

25

HALLIE

Although I couldn't wait to see Ford again in person, a part of me would be sad to leave Baldwin's Shore. The town itself had a tired charm, and the Peninsula Resort and Spa was beyond luxurious. Bradley had shown up before breakfast this morning because he couldn't resist trying out the "spa" part, and now I was blessed with freshly manicured nails and unclogged pores since he'd invited me to tag along.

"More coffee?" the waiter asked.

"Yes, please."

The dining room had a view across the sea, all the way to a rock shaped like a turtle where white-capped waves crashed in clouds of spray. A yacht sailed past in the distance. The chef had made me an omelette, and Emmy's plate was piled high with pastries. Ana picked at her fruit, unsmiling. Nothing new there.

"Where's Bradley?" Emmy asked.

"Getting a massage."

"Good. If he stays in the spa, he can't empty the gift shop."

"He mentioned going to that craft store later—the one

where Meli did her painting. Apparently, he checked out the reviews and it's fandabidozi."

Emmy rolled her eyes. "As long as he remembers we've only got one plane."

"What time is Alex's race?"

"It starts at noon, and he's not exactly gonna be pushing for a good time. Don't forget he's doing this under duress—if he jogs rather than walks, we'll be lucky."

"Aw, bad luck. Riverley's gonna be filled with ribbon and paint and glitter…"

"Shut up." Emmy scowled, but I noticed Ana suppressing a rare smile.

"And yarn and fabric and thread and…"

"I'm carrying a gun."

"For me or for Bradley?"

"Trust me, I'm not gonna run out of ammo."

Oh, I believed that.

My omelette was cooked to perfection, and I took another bite. Maybe someday I could take a vacation here with Ford? I'd always dreamed of being able to travel, and now I had the means to afford it as well as the man to do it with. Scotland, Oregon, the week I'd been promised on Emmy and Black's private island… Trips would depend on our caseloads, though. Mine was only going to get heavier.

And I was still curious about the "Mike" mystery, although solving that puzzle would probably be impossible.

Bradley bounced in and headed straight for the buffet. He'd changed into a pair of bright red pants to match his hair, and his black sweater had *J'adore l'amour* written across it in gold script. Aw, cute.

"Penny for them?" Emmy said. "Although if you're plotting a way to keep Bradley from turning my house into Crafts R Us, I'll up it to a fiver."

"I'm just wondering who Mike is."

"Mike?"

"Pinchy's Mike. As in 'don't shoot, Mike.' Remember?"

"Yeah, I remember, but you shouldn't worry about him."

"Aren't you curious?"

"I was, and Black was also curious, which means Mike is no longer a problem."

"What did...?" I started, but Emmy smiled brightly, too brightly, and I quickly shut my mouth. "Oh, right."

"How's the omelette?"

"Uh, it's good. Thanks."

Emmy was gonna lose her mind.

Bradley had stacked hundreds of dollars' worth of craft products into baskets next to the register, and he was still eying up the shelves. Plus it got worse... After spending weeks learning about genetic relationships, I had a suspicion that Bradley might have a secret twin. His name was Paulo, and they were currently discussing crystal beads and oversized balls of yarn. Why didn't Bradley just buy the whole store and be done with it?

Actually, scratch that thought. I didn't want to give him ideas.

Another employee, Darla according to her badge, assured Bradley they could order the yarn in several shades of pink, and it shouldn't take more than two weeks to arrive. Delay or not, I couldn't see Emmy being thrilled with the purchase.

Speak of the devil... The little brass bell over the door jingled, and Emmy appeared. Oh, this promised to be fun. A battle of wills. Bradley wanted to buy feathers and beads and, yes, enough giant yarn to knit not one but five blankets. Emmy didn't want him to buy any of it. I stifled a laugh as I browsed the gift section, eavesdropping on their argument. Who was winning? If I were putting money on it, I'd have to say Bradley.

The Craft Cabin had some gorgeous sculptures of sailboats on display, not cheap, but I wondered if I should take one home for Ford. He brought me little gifts constantly, candy and earrings, wool scarves and novelty coffee mugs. I was never sure how to return the gesture.

Yes, I'd buy him a sculpture. They were made by a local artist, the sign said—Decker Langdon—and each one of them was unique. And while we were browsing, Decker had brought in three more of his pieces on consignment, and *he* was rather unique too.

Hallie, you have a boyfriend now.

The bell rang again, and Ana walked in. Then she walked right out again. I couldn't blame her—Ana was the practical type, probably allergic to sparkles and feathers and all things kitsch. Emmy followed, and I had a feeling she'd made a big mistake. With no supervision, Bradley would just keep on spending.

Should I step in myself? I considered saying something, but it would be a lost cause, wouldn't it? Bradley could be as stubborn as a mule, and nobody came between him and an economy-sized package of stick-on diamantés.

Hey, what the...?

A cat shot through a door at the rear of the store with a dog in hot pursuit, barking. The cat leapt onto the top of a rack in the middle of the store, the dog launched itself at the terrified kitty, and the whole shelving unit crashed to the floor as Bradley shrieked and dove out of the way. Paulo squealed in sympathy, and I couldn't decide whether to laugh or put my head in my hands. Why did trouble keep following me around? Was it contagious? Had I caught the bug from Emmy?

Paulo tried to grab the hissing cat, but beads had scattered all over the floor, and he ended up on his ass instead. The cat jumped to a new perch, and the dog followed, but not with quite the same enthusiasm as before.

Then I saw it.

Blood.

Where had the blood come from?

The dog. The blood was coming from the dog. Had the cat scratched it? No, there was too much for that. Now it was dripping into big splodges, gathering into a pool on the floor as the mutt stared up at its nemesis. Someone needed to take the dog to the veterinarian, and where was its owner?

Aw, hell.

I had the feeling that even if Alex sprinted around the half-marathon course in record time, we wouldn't be leaving Baldwin's Shore anytime soon...

BONUS STORY - GIRLS' NIGHT

If you'd like to find out what happened on girls' night, I've written a short bonus story for members of my reader group. You can join and read here:

www.elise-noble.com/pine4pple

WHAT'S NEXT?

The Blackwood Security story continues in *Secret Weapon*...

As Director of Special Projects for a global security firm, Emmy Black is well acquainted with trouble, but she didn't expect to run into a proverbial nightmare in small-town Oregon. The place is just hills and trees, right? But a quest to help an injured woman soon leaves Emmy fighting for not only her own survival but the lives of many others too.

When Nine came to Baldwin's Shore, the former member of a Russian hit squad had two goals: to hide and to heal. But someone else has the same idea, and the consequences threaten to upend Nine's carefully crafted existence. With the appearance of old friends and enemies as well as a madman intent on provoking a war and—most disturbingly—an unfamiliar feeling that might be love, Nine is left with one burning question: can an assassin ever truly retire?

For more details:
www.elise-noble.com/secret-weapon

As you might have gathered from the blurb, the next instalment of the Blackwood Security story is a crossover with my Baldwin's Shore series, and it also features an old friend of Ana's. *Secret Weapon* contains spoilers for *Ultraviolet* and the Baldwin's Shore books, so I'd strongly suggest reading those first to get maximum enjoyment!

If you enjoyed *Chimera*, please consider leaving a review.

For an author, every review is incredibly important. Not only do they make us feel warm and fuzzy inside, readers consider them when making their decision whether or not to buy a book. Even a line saying you enjoyed the book or what your favourite part was helps a lot.

WANT TO STALK ME?

For updates on my new releases, giveaways, and other random stuff, you can sign up for my newsletter on my website: www.elise-noble.com

If you're on Facebook, you might also like to join Team Blackwood for exclusive giveaways, sneak previews, and book-related chat. Be the first to find out about new stories, and you might even see your name or one of your suggestions make it into print!

And if you'd like to read my books for FREE, you can also find details of how to join my advance review team.

Would you like to join Team Blackwood?

www.elise-noble.com/team-blackwood

facebook.com/EliseNobleAuthor
twitter.com/EliseANoble
instagram.com/elise_noble

END-OF-BOOK STUFF

Where do I start?

Firstly, thanks to *Chimera* for letting me check several items off my writing wishlist.

The year before Covid happened, I visited Edinburgh for a writers' conference in the summer (which is the best time to visit Scotland because the winter is bloody freezing). I'm actually half Scottish, but I hadn't been oop North in years, so I figured it would make a nice holiday. So booked an apartment for a week. Told my other half, and he said it sounded boring *rolls eyes,* so I left him behind and took my mum instead. My mum is full Scottish and was only too happy to spend a week wandering around Edinburgh. And one day, she came back with a little book of Scottish/English translations. "This is for when you write a Scotland book," she told me. So, here it is. Thanks, Mum.

And then there was Nick's little brother... I mentioned him in Gold Rush many, many years ago, and I always wondered what he was like. Now I know. Kind, like Nick, but a bit more into penguins.

Plus we have the hot plumber. Last summer, our boiler broke, and do you know how difficult it is to find a heating engineer who is (a) up to the job and (b) has availability? Tradesmen are the heroes we all need. So, I jokingly said I'd write a book with a hot plumber, and it turned out to not actually be a joke. Maybe Ross and his friends will get more stories in the future, who knows? (I currently have sixty-one other books I want to write on my to-do list, not even kidding, which will take me about a decade).

Finally, I got to find out what happened to Mila Carmody. I first mentioned her in Black is My Heart, which I wrote about five years ago, and she'd been bugging me ever since. She finally has closure, and so do I, although the story didn't quite go the way I'd originally envisaged. But when I read a news article about human chimeras, I immediately thought "that's going in a book someday."

And now here it is.

Tick, tick, tick, tick, tick.

Emmy will be back soon in Secret Weapon, which is another wishlist book. I always wondered what happened to Ana's former comrades, as mentioned in *Ultraviolet*, and now I know that too :)

Big thanks to Nikki for editing and to Abi for designing the cover. Thanks also to Trev the horse who trekked around Swinley Park with me to find just the right bit of forest to stand in for Glendoon Hall's driveway. We got some curious looks from dog walkers that day! Thanks also to Jeff, Renata, Terri, Musi, David, Stacia, Jessica, Nikita, Quenby, and Jody for beta reading, and to John, Lizbeth, and Debi for proof reading <3

Elise

ALSO BY ELISE NOBLE

Blackwood Security

For the Love of Animals (Nate & Carmen - Prequel)

Black is My Heart (Diamond & Snow - Prequel)

Pitch Black

Into the Black

Forever Black

Gold Rush

Gray is My Heart

Neon (novella)

Out of the Blue

Ultraviolet

Glitter (novella)

Red Alert

White Hot

Sphere (novella)

The Scarlet Affair

Spirit (novella)

Quicksilver

The Girl with the Emerald Ring

Red After Dark

When the Shadows Fall

Pretties in Pink

Chimera (2022)

Secret Weapon (Crossover with Baldwin's Shore) (2022)

The Devil and the Deep Blue Sea (TBA)

Blackwood Elements

Oxygen

Lithium

Carbon

Rhodium

Platinum

Lead

Copper

Bronze

Nickel

Hydrogen (2022)

Blackwood UK

Joker in the Pack

Cherry on Top

Roses are Dead

Shallow Graves

Indigo Rain

Pass the Parcel (TBA)

Blackwood Casefiles

Stolen Hearts

Burning Love (TBA)

Baldwin's Shore

Dirty Little Secrets

Secrets, Lies, and Family Ties

Buried Secrets

Secret Weapon (Crossover with Blackwood Security) (2022)

A Secret to Die For (TBA)

Blackstone House

Hard Lines (2022)

Hard Tide (TBA)

The Electi

Cursed

Spooked

Possessed

Demented

Judged

The Planes

A Vampire in Vegas

A Devil in the Dark (TBA)

The Trouble Series

Trouble in Paradise

Nothing but Trouble

24 Hours of Trouble

Standalone

Life

Coco du Ciel

A Very Happy Christmas (novella)

Twisted (short stories)

Books with clean versions available (no swearing and no on-the-page sex)

Pitch Black

Into the Black

Forever Black

Gold Rush

Gray is My Heart

Audiobooks

Black is My Heart (Diamond & Snow - Prequel)

Pitch Black

Into the Black

Forever Black

Gold Rush

Gray is My Heart

Neon (novella)

Made in the USA
Middletown, DE
19 February 2025

71556430R00111